PAPERCUTZ SLICES

THE HUNGER PAINS

PAPER

PAPERCUTZ™ SLICES

Graphic Novels Available from PAPERCUTZ™ (Who else..?!)

PAPERCUTZ SLICES
AN ALL-NEW, UNAUTHORIZED PARODY!
Harry Potty
AND THE DEATHLY BORING
STEFAN PETRUCHA
RICK PARKER
PAPERCUTZ

Graphic Novel #1
"Harry Potty and the Deathly Boring"

PAPERCUTZ SLICES
AN ALL-NEW, UNAUTHORIZED PARODY
breaking down
STEFAN PETRUCHA & RICK PARKER
AUTHORS OF "DIARY OF A STINKY DEAD KID" AND "HARRY POTTY"
PAPERCUTZ

Graphic Novel #2
"breaking down"

PAPERCUTZ SLICES
AN ALL-NEW UNAUTHORIZED PARODY
PERCY JERKSON
& THE OVOLACTOVEGETARIANS
PAPERCUTZ

Graphic Novel #3
"Percy Jerkson & The Ovolactovegetarians"

PAPERCUTZ SLICES
AN ALL-NEW UNAUTHORIZED PARODY
THE HUNGER PAINS
Stefan
PETRUCHA
Rick
PARKER
PAPERCUTZ

Graphic Novel #4
"The Hunger Pains"

NEW! PAPERCUTZ™ SLICES is now available from COMIXOLOGY™

Now you can read PAPERCUTZ SLICES and look like you're conducting serious business!

PAPERCUTZ SLICES graphic novels are available at booksellers everywhere. At bookstores, comicbook stores, online, out of the trunk in the back of Rick Parker's car, and who knows where else? If you still are unable to find PAPERCUTZ SLICES (probably because it sold out) you can always order directly from Papercutz—but it'll cost you! PAPERCUTZ SLICES is available in paperback for $6.99 each; in hardcover for $10.99 each. But that's not the worst part-- please add $4.00 for postage and handling for the first book, and add $1.00 for each additional book. Going to your favorite bookseller, buying online, or even getting a copy from your local library doesn't seem so bad now, does it? But if you still insist on ordering from Papercutz, and just to make everything just a little bit more complicated, please make your check payable to NBM Publishing. Don't ask why—it's just how it works. Send to: Papercutz, 40 Exchange Place, Ste. 1308, New York, NY 10005 Or call 800 886 1223 (9-6 EST M-F) MC-Visa-Amex accepted

www.papercutz.com

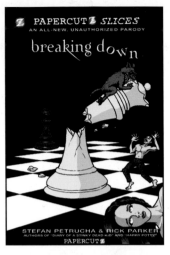

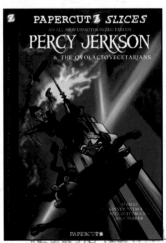

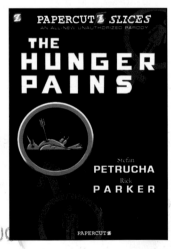

PAPERCUT乙™ SLICES

#4 THE HUNGER PAINS

Stefan
PETRUCHA
Writer

Rick
PARKER
Artist

PAPERCUT乙™
New York

"THE HUNGER PAINS"

STEFAN PETRUCHA – Writer
RICK PARKER – Artist, Colorist, Letterer

NELSON DESIGN GROUP, LLC
Production

MICHAEL PETRANEK
Associate Editor

JIM SALICRUP
Editor-in-Chief

ISBN: 978-1-59707-312-7 paperback edition
ISBN: 978-1-59707-313-4 hardcover edition

Printed in China
February 2012 by New Era Printing, LTD
Trend Centre, 29-31 Cheung Lee St.
Chaiwan, Hong Kong

Distributed by Macmillan
First Printing

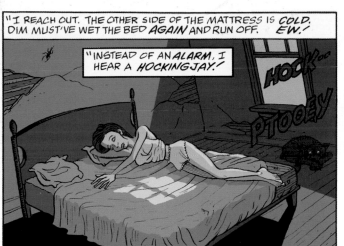

"I REACH OUT. THE OTHER SIDE OF THE MATTRESS IS *COLD*. DIM MUST'VE WET THE BED *AGAIN* AND RUN OFF. *EW!*"

"INSTEAD OF AN *ALARM*, I HEAR A *HOCKINGJAY!*"

"KIND OF HARD *NOT* TO HEAR THEM."

"YEARS AGO, THE *GOVERNMENT* CROSS-BRED *HOCKEY PLAYERS* WITH *JAYBIRDS* HOPING FOR *FLYING SOLDIERS.*"

"INSTEAD, ALL THEY DO IS *SPIT!*"

"THE GOVERNMENT ISN'T VERY *BRIGHT.*"

"NEITHER IS MY SISTER'S CAT, *BUTTERBUTT.* INSTEAD OF CHASING THE BIRD, SHE JUST LIES THERE, COMPLETELY *USELESS!*"

"WELL, MAYBE NOT *COMPLETELY.*"

MEEOWRRR...?

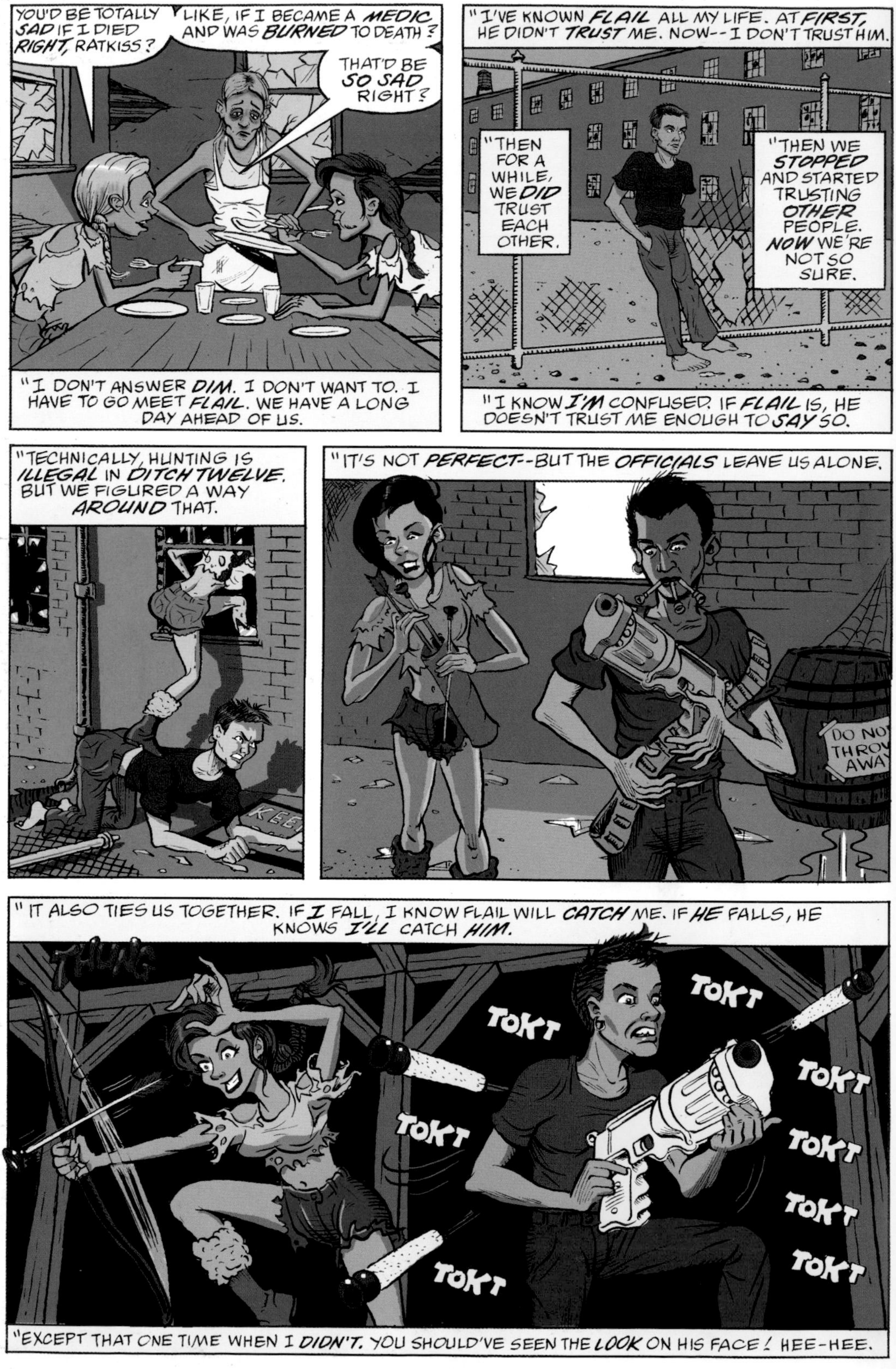

YOU'D BE TOTALLY SAD IF I DIED RIGHT, RATKISS?
LIKE, IF I BECAME A MEDIC AND WAS BURNED TO DEATH?
THAT'D BE SO SAD RIGHT?
"I DON'T ANSWER DIM. I DON'T WANT TO. I HAVE TO GO MEET FLAIL. WE HAVE A LONG DAY AHEAD OF US.
"I'VE KNOWN FLAIL ALL MY LIFE. AT FIRST, HE DIDN'T TRUST ME. NOW-- I DON'T TRUST HIM.
"THEN FOR A WHILE, WE DID TRUST EACH OTHER.
"THEN WE STOPPED AND STARTED TRUSTING OTHER PEOPLE. NOW WE'RE NOT SO SURE.
"I KNOW I'M CONFUSED. IF FLAIL IS, HE DOESN'T TRUST ME ENOUGH TO SAY SO.
"TECHNICALLY, HUNTING IS ILLEGAL IN DITCH TWELVE. BUT WE FIGURED A WAY AROUND THAT.
"IT'S NOT PERFECT--BUT THE OFFICIALS LEAVE US ALONE.
"IT ALSO TIES US TOGETHER. IF I FALL, I KNOW FLAIL WILL CATCH ME. IF HE FALLS, HE KNOWS I'LL CATCH HIM.
TOKT
TOKT
TOKT
TOKT
TOKT
TOKT
TOKT
TOKT
"EXCEPT THAT ONE TIME WHEN I DIDN'T. YOU SHOULD'VE SEEN THE LOOK ON HIS FACE! HEE-HEE.

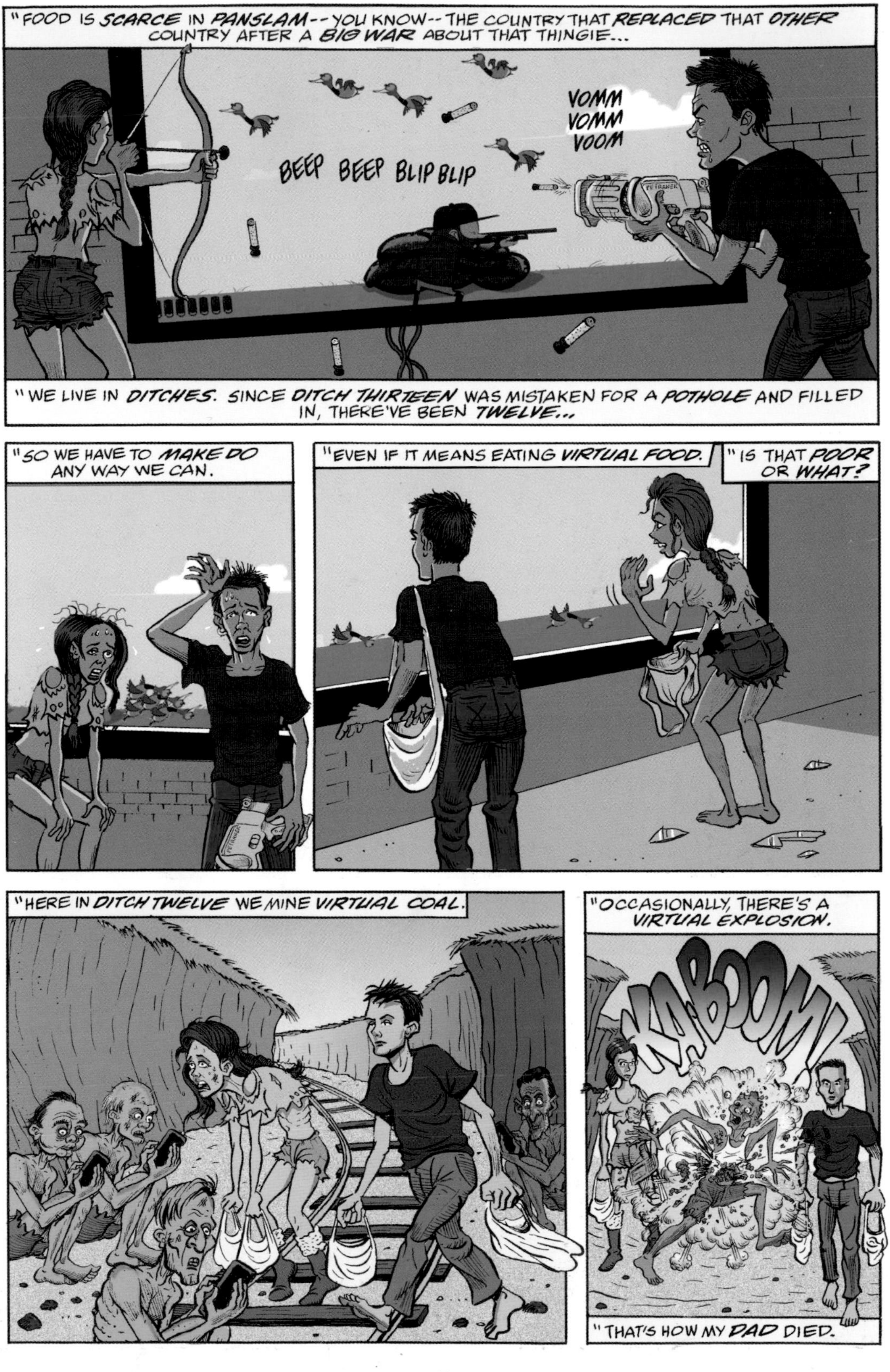
"FOOD IS SCARCE IN PANSLAM-- YOU KNOW-- THE COUNTRY THAT REPLACED THAT OTHER COUNTRY AFTER A BIG WAR ABOUT THAT THINGIE...
BEEP BEEP BLIP BLIP
VOMM VOMM VOOM
"WE LIVE IN DITCHES. SINCE DITCH THIRTEEN WAS MISTAKEN FOR A POTHOLE AND FILLED IN, THERE'VE BEEN TWELVE...
"SO WE HAVE TO MAKE DO ANY WAY WE CAN.
"EVEN IF IT MEANS EATING VIRTUAL FOOD.
"IS THAT POOR OR WHAT?
"HERE IN DITCH TWELVE WE MINE VIRTUAL COAL.
"OCCASIONALLY, THERE'S A VIRTUAL EXPLOSION.
KA-BOOM!
"THAT'S HOW MY DAD DIED.

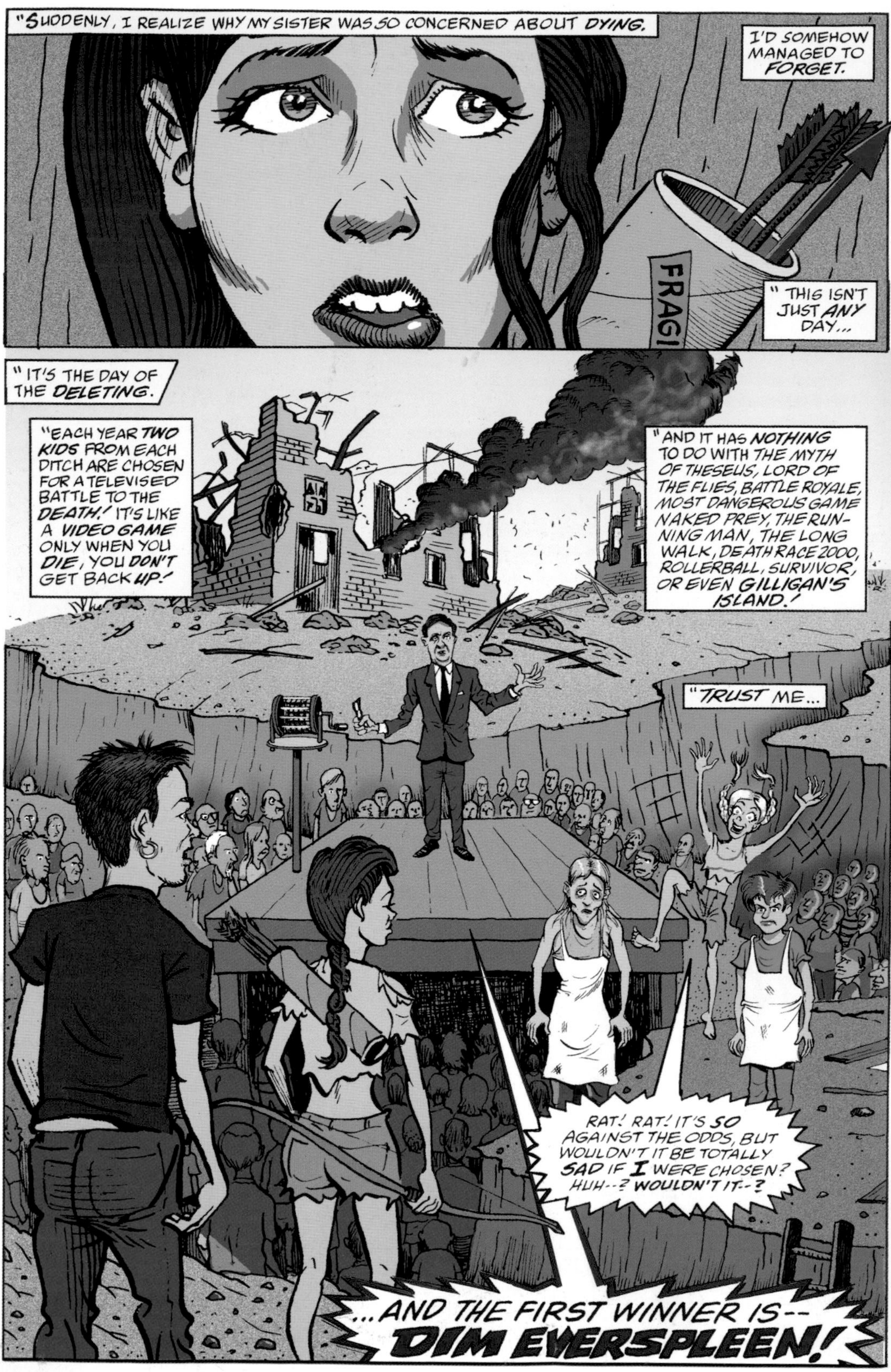
"SUDDENLY, I REALIZE WHY MY SISTER WAS SO CONCERNED ABOUT DYING.
I'D SOMEHOW MANAGED TO FORGET.
FRAGI
"THIS ISN'T JUST ANY DAY...
"IT'S THE DAY OF THE DELETING.
"EACH YEAR TWO KIDS FROM EACH DITCH ARE CHOSEN FOR A TELEVISED BATTLE TO THE DEATH! IT'S LIKE A VIDEO GAME ONLY WHEN YOU DIE, YOU DON'T GET BACK UP!
"AND IT HAS NOTHING TO DO WITH THE MYTH OF THESEUS, LORD OF THE FLIES, BATTLE ROYALE, MOST DANGEROUS GAME NAKED PREY, THE RUNNING MAN, THE LONG WALK, DEATH RACE 2000, ROLLERBALL, SURVIVOR, OR EVEN GILLIGAN'S ISLAND!
"TRUST ME...
RAT! RAT! IT'S SO AGAINST THE ODDS, BUT WOULDN'T IT BE TOTALLY SAD IF I WERE CHOSEN? HUH--? WOULDN'T IT--?
...AND THE FIRST WINNER IS-- DIM EVERSPLEEN!

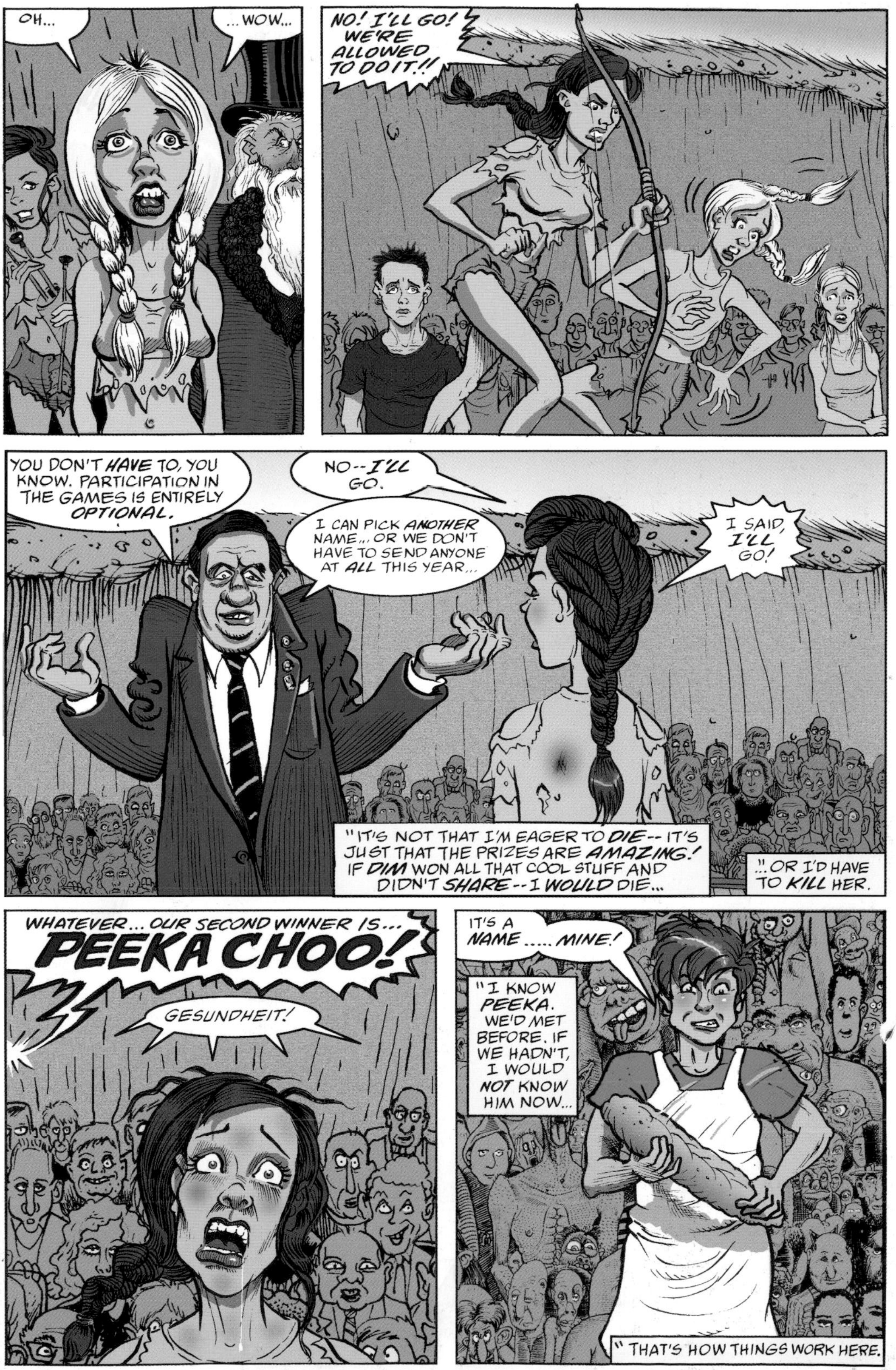

OH...
...WOW...
NO! I'LL GO! WE'RE ALLOWED TO DO IT!!
YOU DON'T HAVE TO, YOU KNOW. PARTICIPATION IN THE GAMES IS ENTIRELY OPTIONAL.
NO--I'LL GO.
I CAN PICK ANOTHER NAME... OR WE DON'T HAVE TO SEND ANYONE AT ALL THIS YEAR...
I SAID, I'LL GO!
"IT'S NOT THAT I'M EAGER TO DIE-- IT'S JUST THAT THE PRIZES ARE AMAZING! IF DIM WON ALL THAT COOL STUFF AND DIDN'T SHARE--I WOULD DIE...
"...OR I'D HAVE TO KILL HER.
WHATEVER... OUR SECOND WINNER IS... PEEKA CHOO!
GESUNDHEIT!
IT'S A NAME..... MINE!
"I KNOW PEEKA. WE'D MET BEFORE. IF WE HADN'T, I WOULD NOT KNOW HIM NOW...
"THAT'S HOW THINGS WORK HERE.

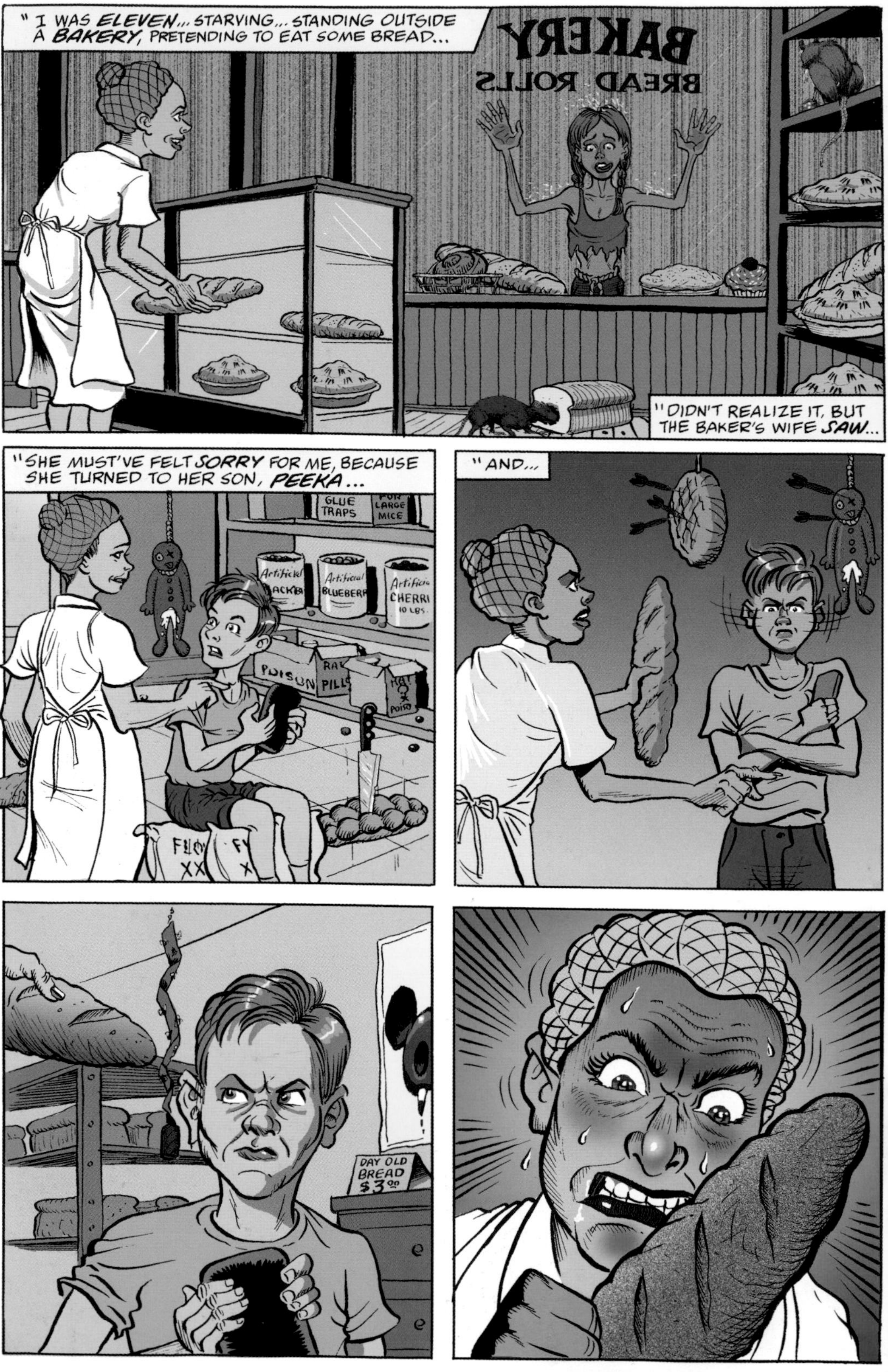
"I WAS ELEVEN... STARVING... STANDING OUTSIDE A BAKERY, PRETENDING TO EAT SOME BREAD...
BAKERY
BREAD ROLLS
"DIDN'T REALIZE IT, BUT THE BAKER'S WIFE SAW...
"SHE MUST'VE FELT SORRY FOR ME, BECAUSE SHE TURNED TO HER SON, PEEKA...
GLUE TRAPS
FOR LARGE MICE
Artificial BLUEBERR
Artificia CHERRI 10 LBS.
POISON
RAT PILLS
"AND...
DAY OLD BREAD $3.00

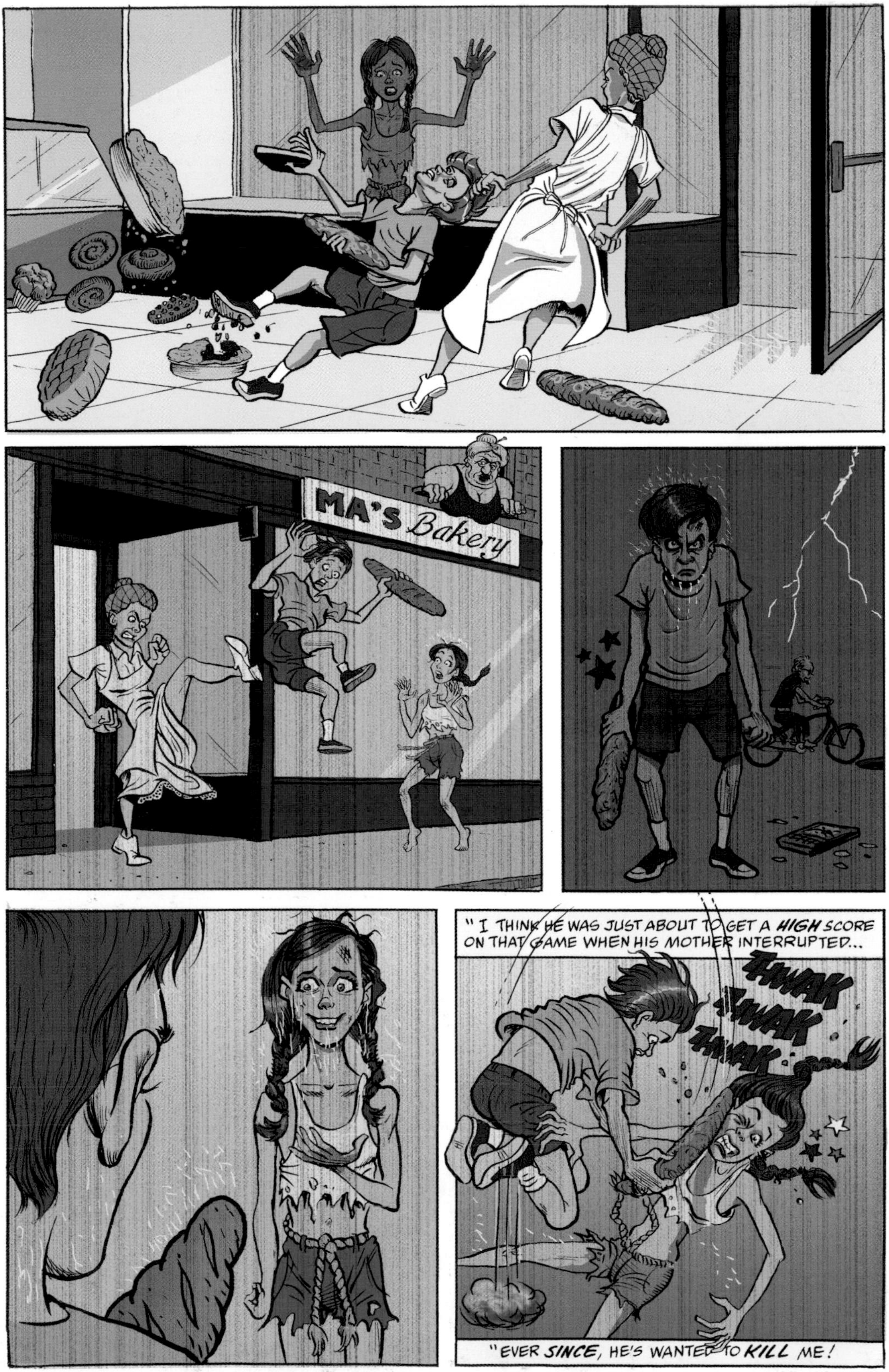
MA'S Bakery
" I THINK HE WAS JUST ABOUT TO GET A HIGH SCORE ON THAT GAME WHEN HIS MOTHER INTERRUPTED...
THWAK
THWAK
THWAK
" EVER SINCE, HE'S WANTED TO KILL ME!

"AS PART OF OUR *TRAINING*, WE'RE TO BE ADVISED BY A PRIOR *WINNER*...

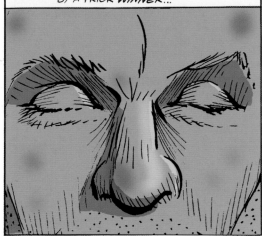

"*HEYBITCH BLUBBERNASTY* WAS DITCH TWELVE'S *ONLY* WINNER...

"NO ONE WAS QUITE SURE *HOW* HE WON...

"AFTER STANDING OVER HIM FOR AN *HOUR*, I THOUGHT MAYBE *THIS* WAS HIS WAY OF TEACHING US, THAT HE WAS *SHOWING* US HIS STRATEGY.

"HOW HE'D WON THE GAMES--BY PLAYING *DEAD!*

"OR MAYBE HE *WAS* DEAD...

"...IT WAS HARD TO *TELL!*

"WHEN PEEKA POKES HIM WITH A STICK, I START THINKING HE'S NOT SO *BAD*--FOR SOMEONE WHO WANTS TO *KILL* ME.

"WE STOOD THERE TOGETHER FOR A *WHILE*-- POKING HEYBITCH WITH STICKS--THEN *LEFT*...

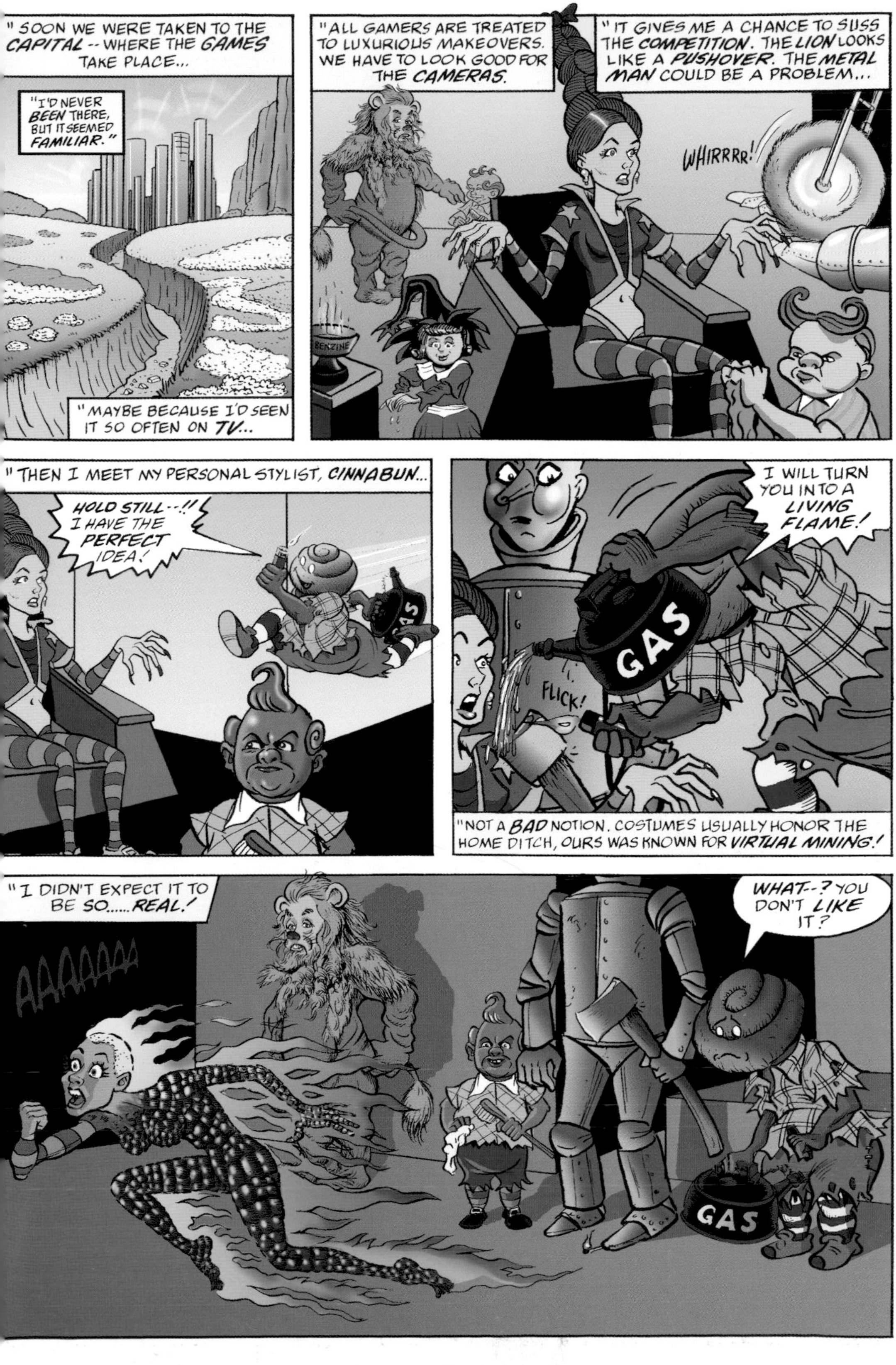
"SOON WE WERE TAKEN TO THE CAPITAL -- WHERE THE GAMES TAKE PLACE...
"I'D NEVER BEEN THERE, BUT IT SEEMED FAMILIAR."
"MAYBE BECAUSE I'D SEEN IT SO OFTEN ON TV...
"ALL GAMERS ARE TREATED TO LUXURIOUS MAKEOVERS. WE HAVE TO LOOK GOOD FOR THE CAMERAS.
"IT GIVES ME A CHANCE TO SUSS THE COMPETITION. THE LION LOOKS LIKE A PUSHOVER. THE METAL MAN COULD BE A PROBLEM...
WHIRRRR!
BENZINE
"THEN I MEET MY PERSONAL STYLIST, CINNABUN...
HOLD STILL--!! I HAVE THE PERFECT IDEA!
I WILL TURN YOU INTO A LIVING FLAME!
GAS
FLICK!
"NOT A BAD NOTION. COSTUMES USUALLY HONOR THE HOME DITCH, OURS WAS KNOWN FOR VIRTUAL MINING!
"I DIDN'T EXPECT IT TO BE SO...... REAL!
AAAAAA
WHAT--? YOU DON'T LIKE IT?
GAS

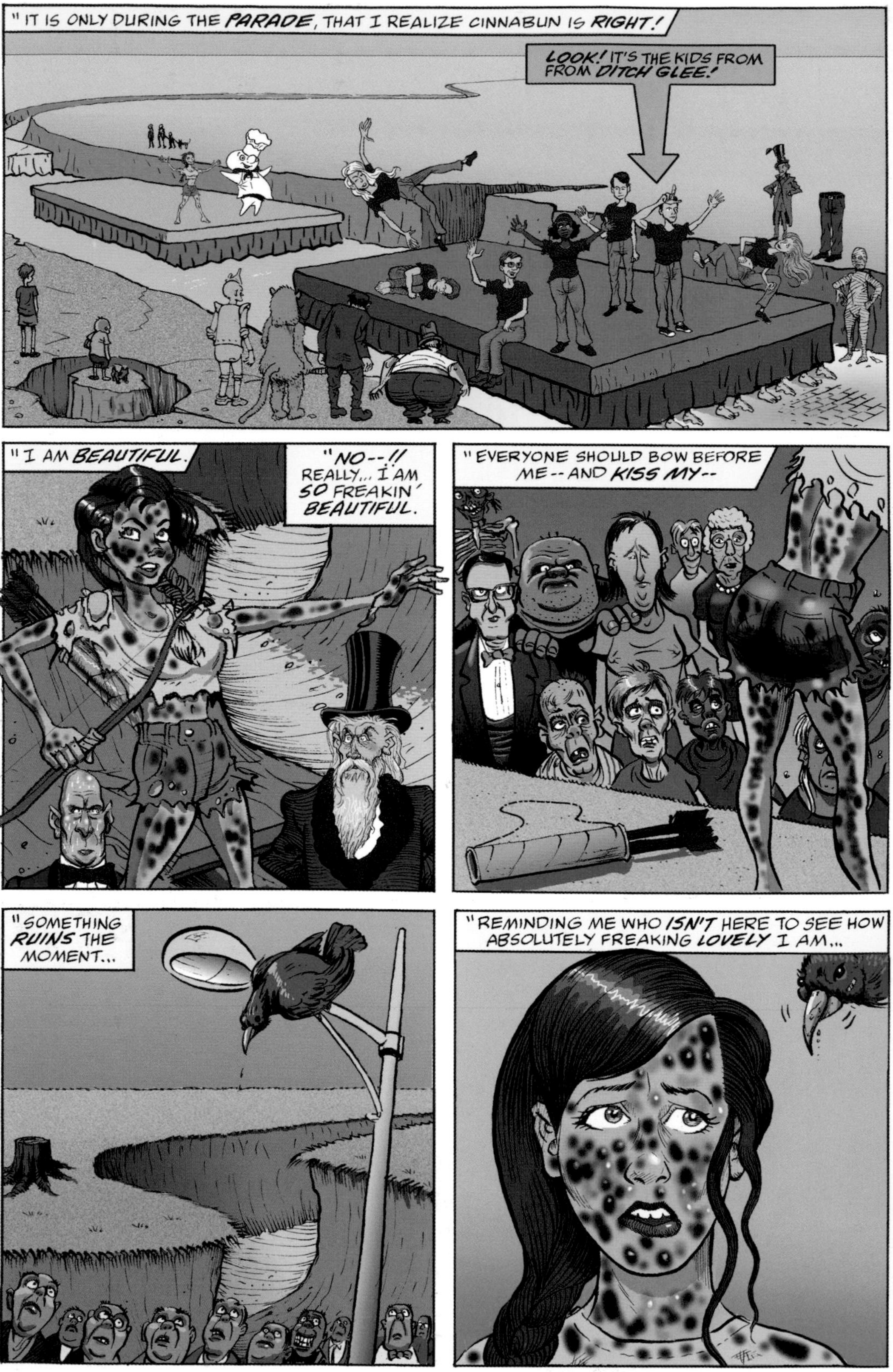
"IT IS ONLY DURING THE PARADE, THAT I REALIZE CINNABUN IS RIGHT!
LOOK! IT'S THE KIDS FROM FROM DITCH GLEE!
"I AM BEAUTIFUL.
"NO--!! REALLY... I AM SO FREAKIN' BEAUTIFUL.
"EVERYONE SHOULD BOW BEFORE ME -- AND KISS MY--
"SOMETHING RUINS THE MOMENT...
"REMINDING ME WHO ISN'T HERE TO SEE HOW ABSOLUTELY FREAKING LOVELY I AM...

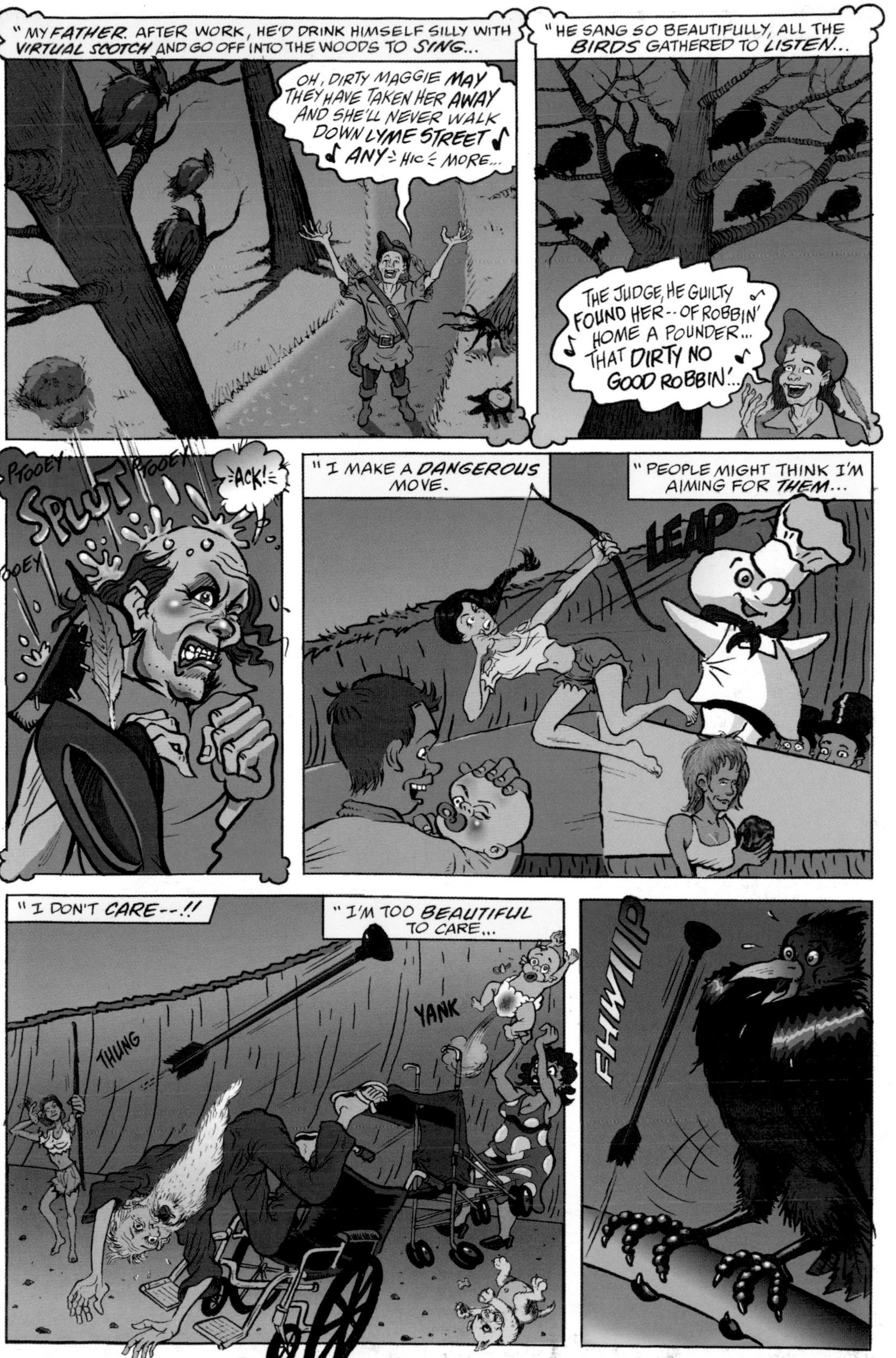

"MY FATHER. AFTER WORK, HE'D DRINK HIMSELF SILLY WITH VIRTUAL SCOTCH AND GO OFF INTO THE WOODS TO SING...
OH, DIRTY MAGGIE MAY THEY HAVE TAKEN HER AWAY AND SHE'LL NEVER WALK DOWN LYME STREET ANY HIC MORE...
"HE SANG SO BEAUTIFULLY, ALL THE BIRDS GATHERED TO LISTEN...
THE JUDGE, HE GUILTY FOUND HER-- OF ROBBIN' HOME A POUNDER... THAT DIRTY NO GOOD ROBBIN'...
PTOOEY
SPLUT
PTOOEY
ACK!
PTOOEY
"I MAKE A DANGEROUS MOVE.
"PEOPLE MIGHT THINK I'M AIMING FOR THEM...
LEAP
"I DON'T CARE--!!
"I'M TOO BEAUTIFUL TO CARE...
YANK
THUNG
FHWIIP

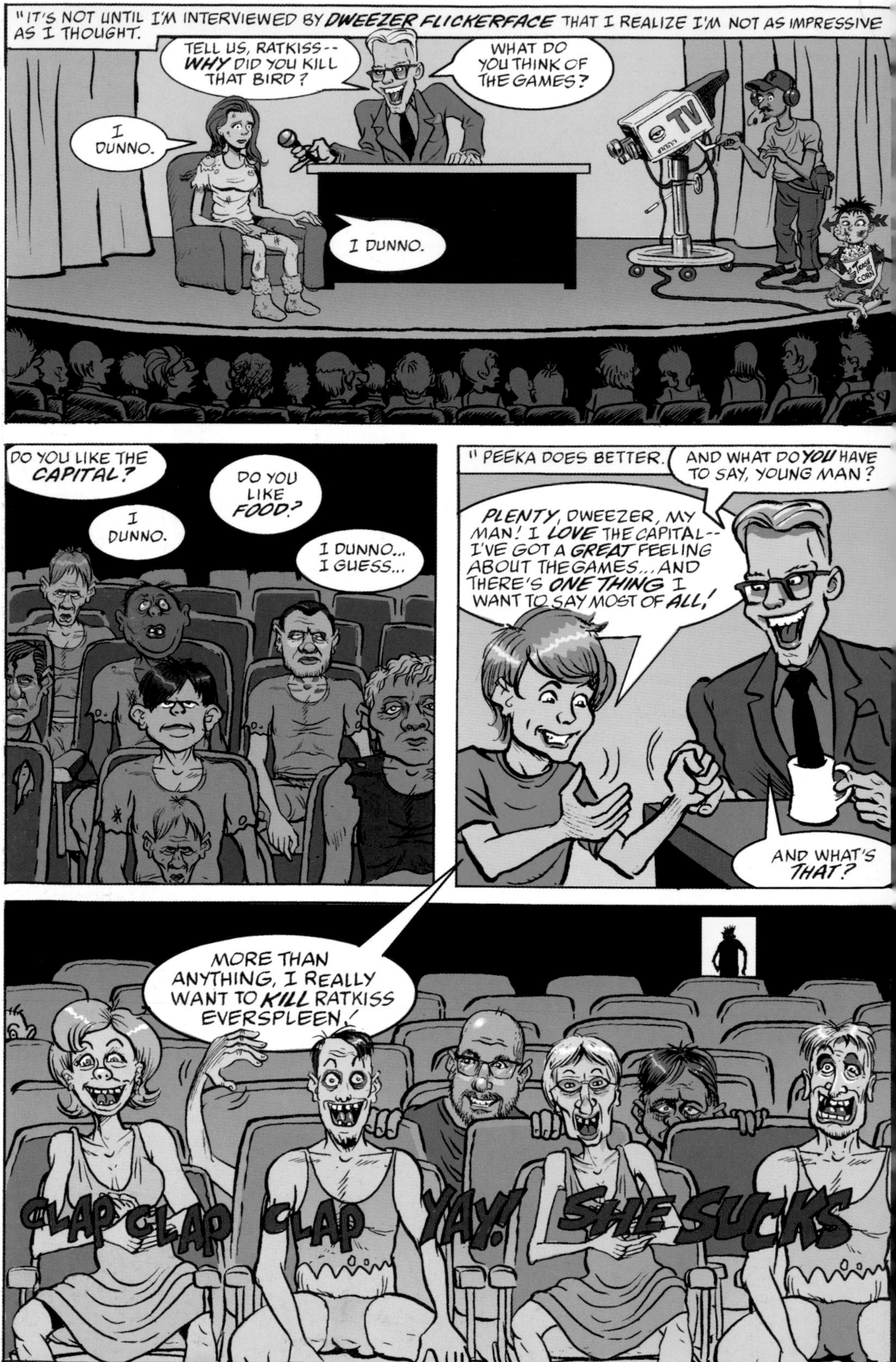

"IT'S NOT UNTIL I'M INTERVIEWED BY DWEEZER FLICKERFACE THAT I REALIZE I'M NOT AS IMPRESSIVE AS I THOUGHT.
TELL US, RATKISS-- WHY DID YOU KILL THAT BIRD?
I DUNNO.
WHAT DO YOU THINK OF THE GAMES?
I DUNNO.
DO YOU LIKE THE CAPITAL?
I DUNNO.
DO YOU LIKE FOOD?
I DUNNO... I GUESS...
"PEEKA DOES BETTER.
AND WHAT DO YOU HAVE TO SAY, YOUNG MAN?
PLENTY, DWEEZER, MY MAN! I LOVE THE CAPITAL-- I'VE GOT A GREAT FEELING ABOUT THE GAMES... AND THERE'S ONE THING I WANT TO SAY MOST OF ALL!
AND WHAT'S THAT?
MORE THAN ANYTHING, I REALLY WANT TO KILL RATKISS EVERSPLEEN!
CLAP CLAP CLAP YAY! SHE SUCKS

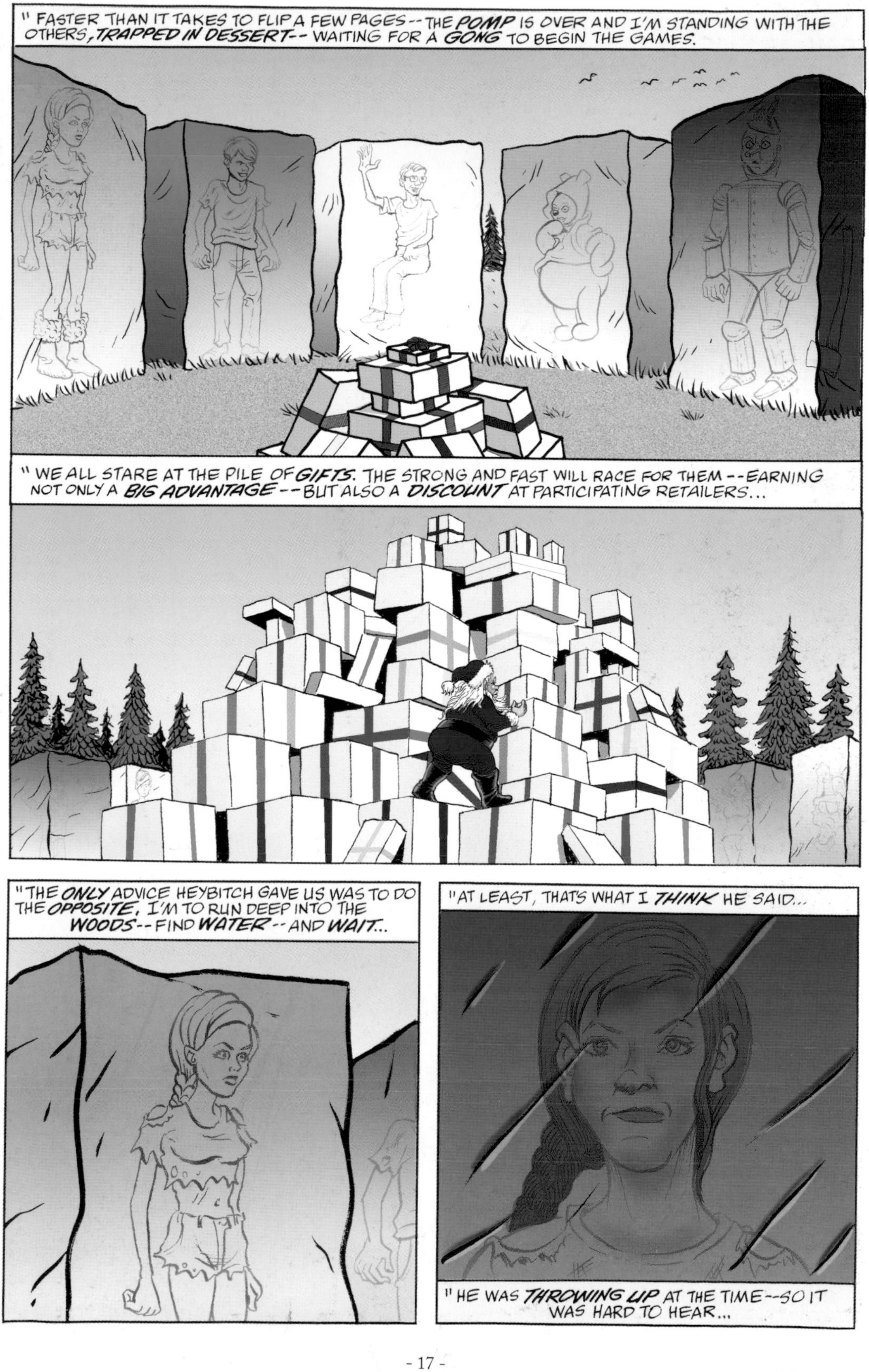
"FASTER THAN IT TAKES TO FLIP A FEW PAGES--THE POMP IS OVER AND I'M STANDING WITH THE OTHERS, TRAPPED IN DESSERT-- WAITING FOR A GONG TO BEGIN THE GAMES.
"WE ALL STARE AT THE PILE OF GIFTS. THE STRONG AND FAST WILL RACE FOR THEM--EARNING NOT ONLY A BIG ADVANTAGE--BUT ALSO A DISCOUNT AT PARTICIPATING RETAILERS...
"THE ONLY ADVICE HEYBITCH GAVE US WAS TO DO THE OPPOSITE. I'M TO RUN DEEP INTO THE WOODS--FIND WATER--AND WAIT...
"AT LEAST, THAT'S WHAT I THINK HE SAID...
"HE WAS THROWING UP AT THE TIME--SO IT WAS HARD TO HEAR...

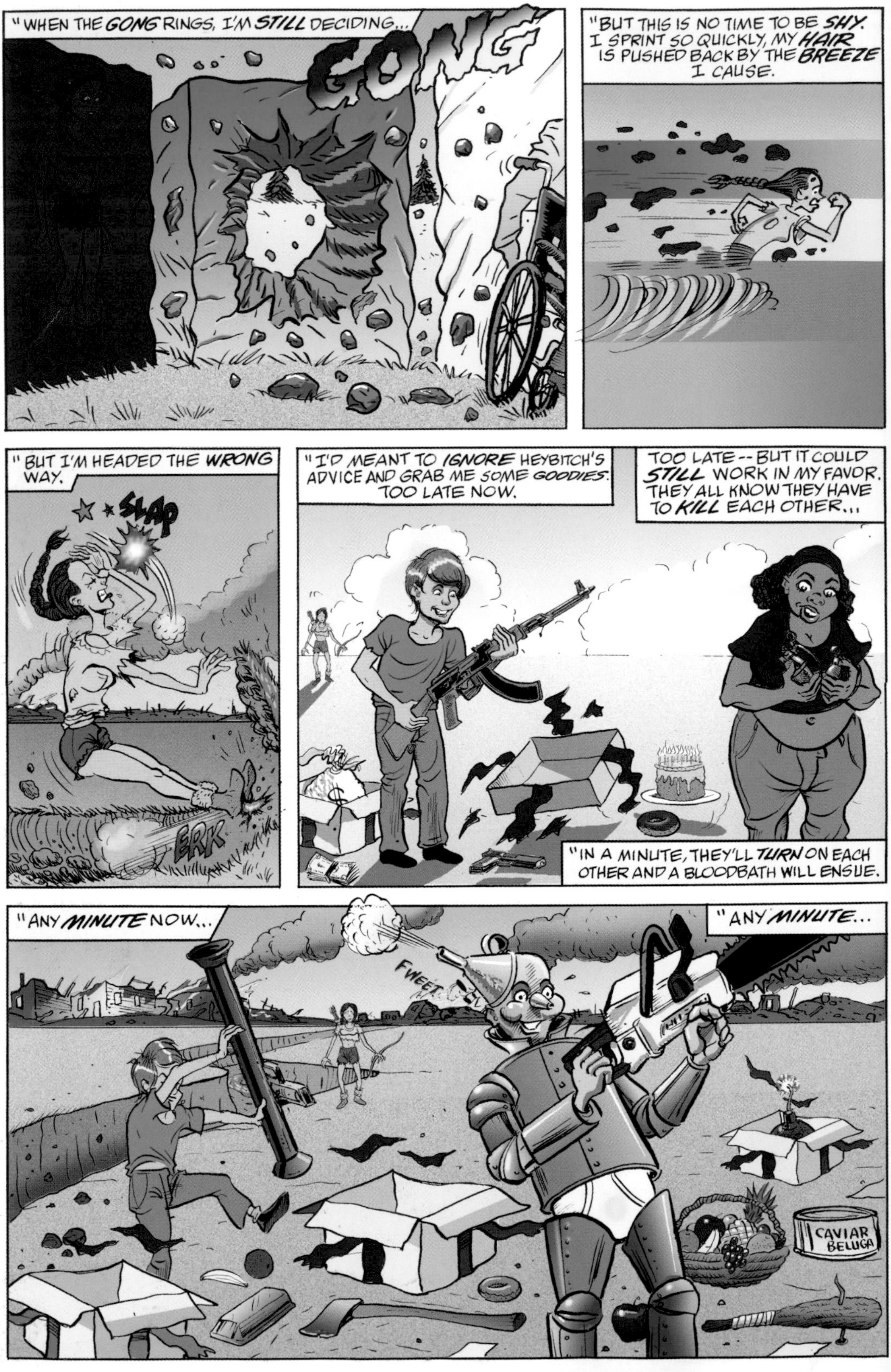
"WHEN THE GONG RINGS, I'M STILL DECIDING...
GONG
"BUT THIS IS NO TIME TO BE SHY. I SPRINT SO QUICKLY, MY HAIR IS PUSHED BACK BY THE BREEZE I CAUSE.
"BUT I'M HEADED THE WRONG WAY.
SLAP
ERK
"I'D MEANT TO IGNORE HEYBITCH'S ADVICE AND GRAB ME SOME GOODIES. TOO LATE NOW.
TOO LATE -- BUT IT COULD STILL WORK IN MY FAVOR. THEY ALL KNOW THEY HAVE TO KILL EACH OTHER...
"IN A MINUTE, THEY'LL TURN ON EACH OTHER AND A BLOODBATH WILL ENSUE.
"ANY MINUTE NOW...
"ANY MINUTE...
FWEET
CAVIAR BELUGA

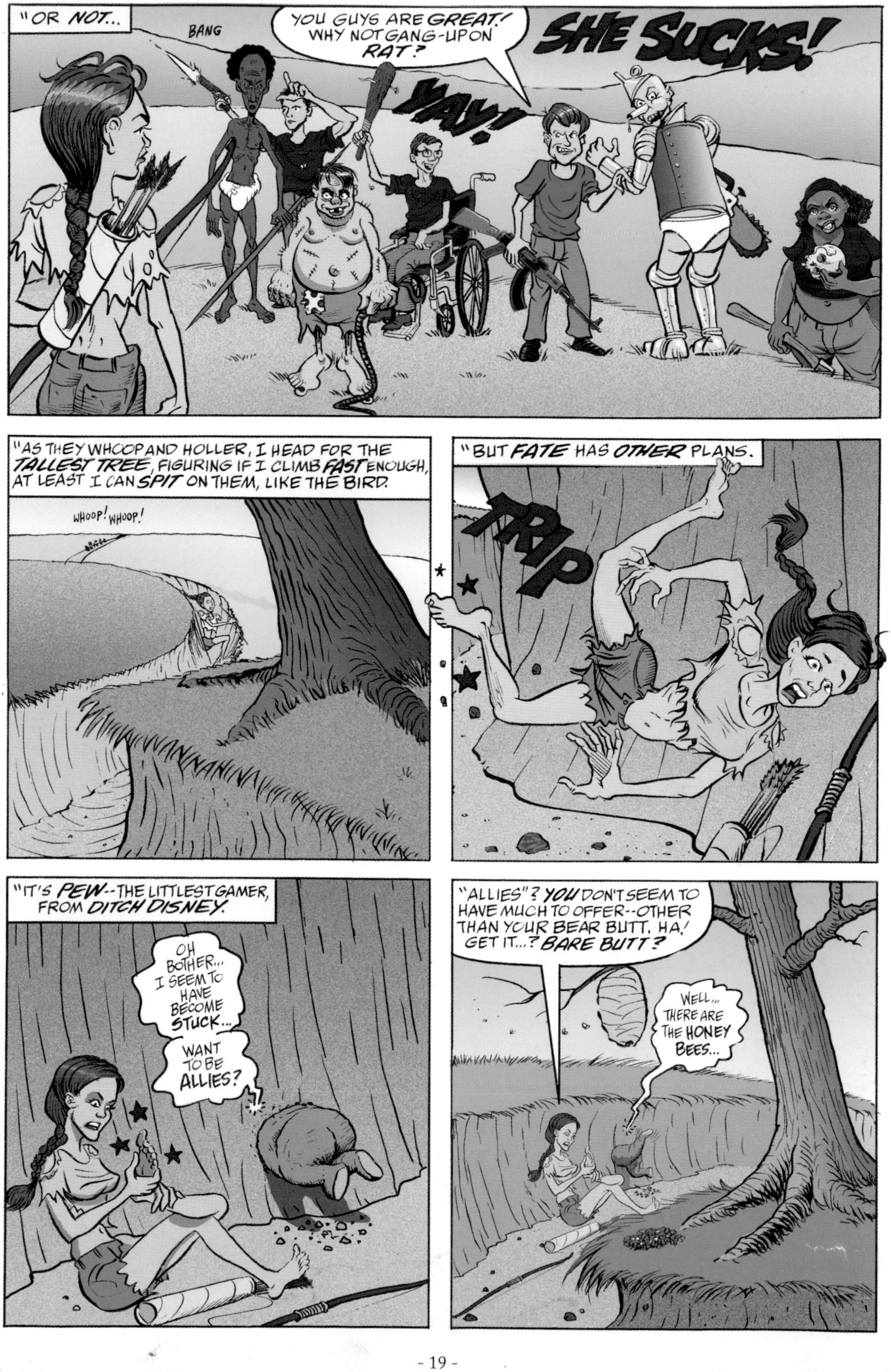
"OR NOT...
BANG
YOU GUYS ARE GREAT! WHY NOT GANG-UP ON RAT?
YAY!
SHE SUCKS!
"AS THEY WHOOP AND HOLLER, I HEAD FOR THE TALLEST TREE, FIGURING IF I CLIMB FAST ENOUGH, AT LEAST I CAN SPIT ON THEM, LIKE THE BIRD.
WHOOP! WHOOP!
"BUT FATE HAS OTHER PLANS.
TRIP
"IT'S PEW--THE LITTLEST GAMER, FROM DITCH DISNEY.
OH BOTHER... I SEEM TO HAVE BECOME STUCK...
WANT TO BE ALLIES?
"ALLIES"? YOU DON'T SEEM TO HAVE MUCH TO OFFER--OTHER THAN YOUR BEAR BUTT. HA! GET IT...? BARE BUTT?
WELL... THERE ARE THE HONEY BEES...

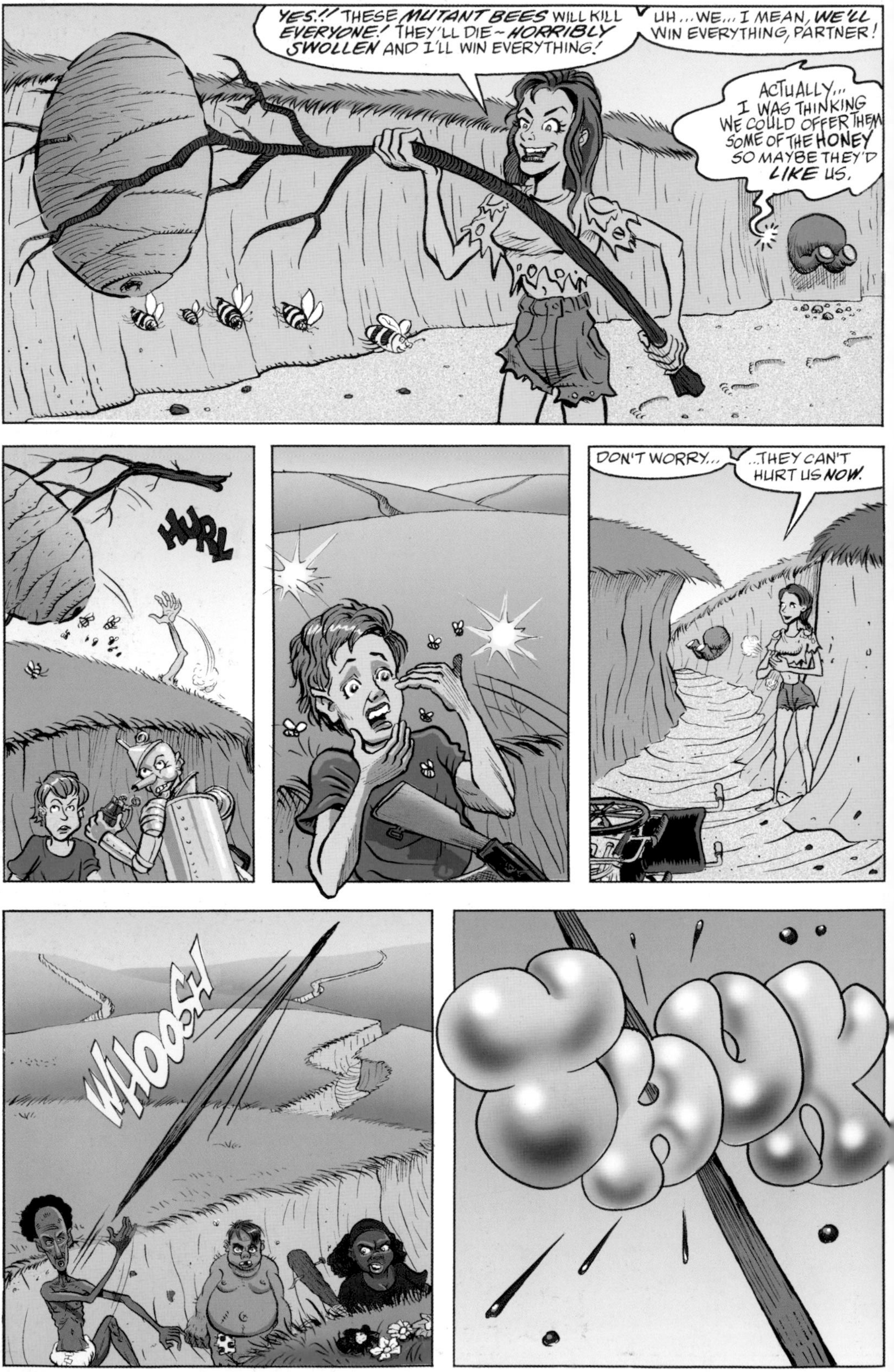

YES!! THESE MUTANT BEES WILL KILL EVERYONE! THEY'LL DIE~HORRIBLY SWOLLEN AND I'LL WIN EVERYTHING!
UH... WE... I MEAN, WE'LL WIN EVERYTHING, PARTNER!
ACTUALLY... I WAS THINKING WE COULD OFFER THEM SOME OF THE HONEY SO MAYBE THEY'D LIKE US.
HURL
DON'T WORRY...
...THEY CAN'T HURT US NOW.
WHOOSH

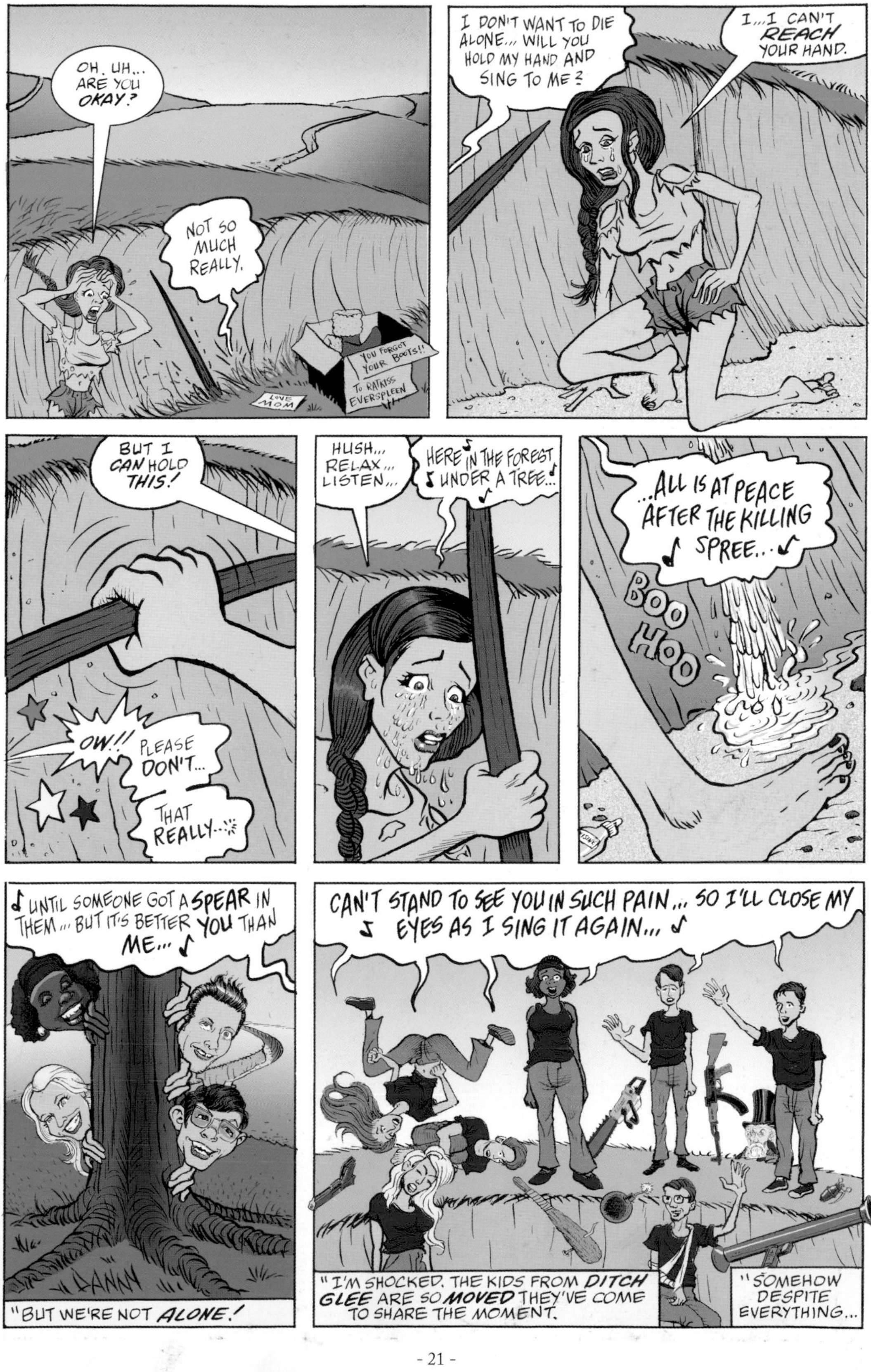

OH, UH... ARE YOU OKAY?
NOT SO MUCH REALLY.
YOU FORGOT YOUR BOOTS!!
TO RATKISS EVERSPLEEN
LOVE MOM
I DON'T WANT TO DIE ALONE... WILL YOU HOLD MY HAND AND SING TO ME?
I... I CAN'T REACH YOUR HAND.
BUT I CAN HOLD THIS!
OW!!
PLEASE DON'T...
THAT REALLY...
HUSH... RELAX... LISTEN...
HERE IN THE FOREST UNDER A TREE...
...ALL IS AT PEACE AFTER THE KILLING SPREE...
BOO HOO
UNTIL SOMEONE GOT A SPEAR IN THEM... BUT IT'S BETTER YOU THAN ME...
"BUT WE'RE NOT ALONE!
CAN'T STAND TO SEE YOU IN SUCH PAIN... SO I'LL CLOSE MY EYES AS I SING IT AGAIN...
"I'M SHOCKED. THE KIDS FROM DITCH GLEE ARE SO MOVED THEY'VE COME TO SHARE THE MOMENT.
"SOMEHOW DESPITE EVERYTHING...

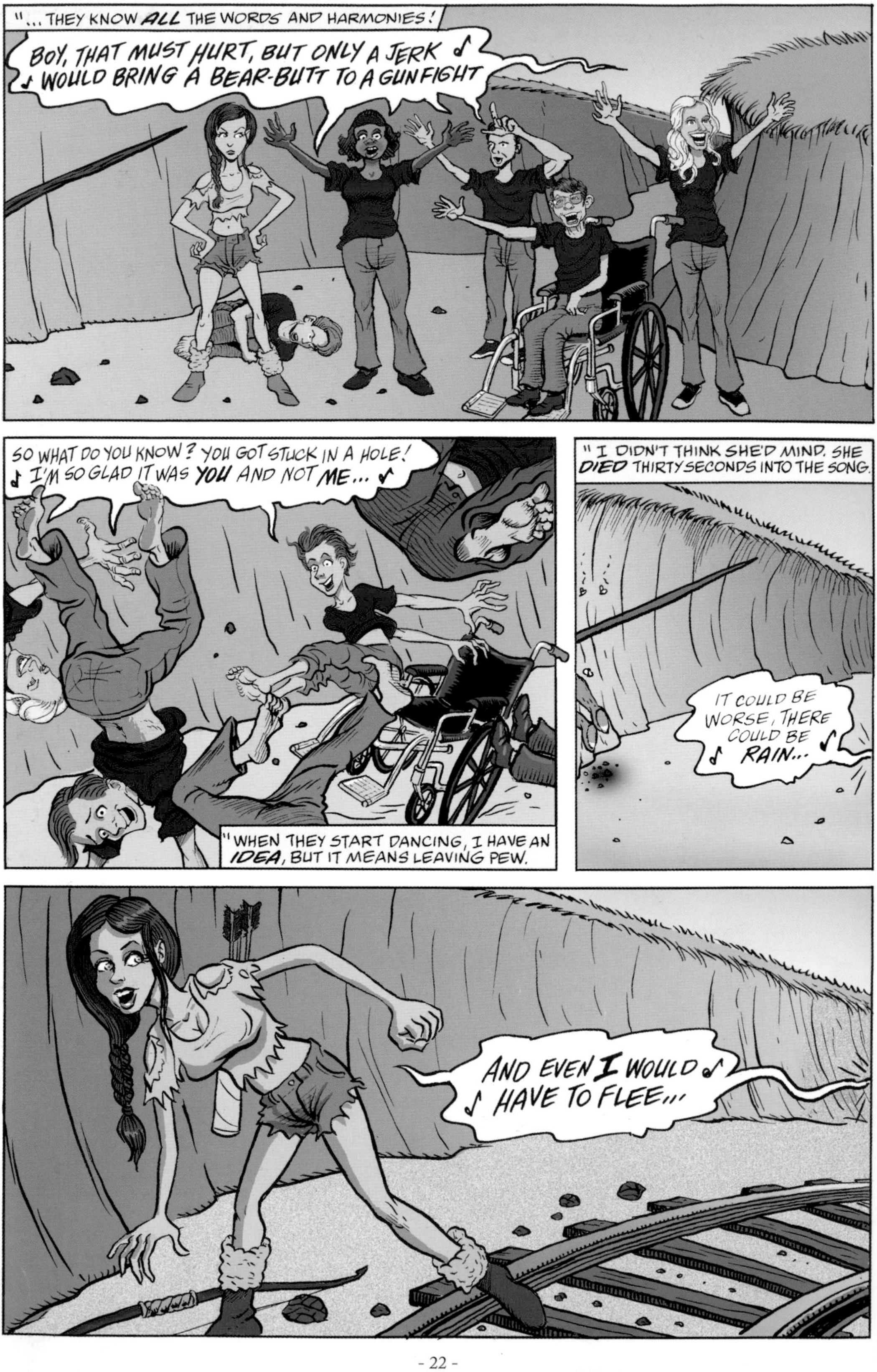
"... THEY KNOW ALL THE WORDS AND HARMONIES!
BOY, THAT MUST HURT, BUT ONLY A JERK ♪ ♪ WOULD BRING A BEAR-BUTT TO A GUNFIGHT
SO WHAT DO YOU KNOW? YOU GOT STUCK IN A HOLE! ♪ I'M SO GLAD IT WAS YOU AND NOT ME... ♪
"WHEN THEY START DANCING, I HAVE AN IDEA, BUT IT MEANS LEAVING PEW.
"I DIDN'T THINK SHE'D MIND. SHE DIED THIRTY SECONDS INTO THE SONG.
IT COULD BE WORSE, THERE COULD BE ♪ RAIN... ♪
AND EVEN I WOULD ♪ ♪ HAVE TO FLEE...

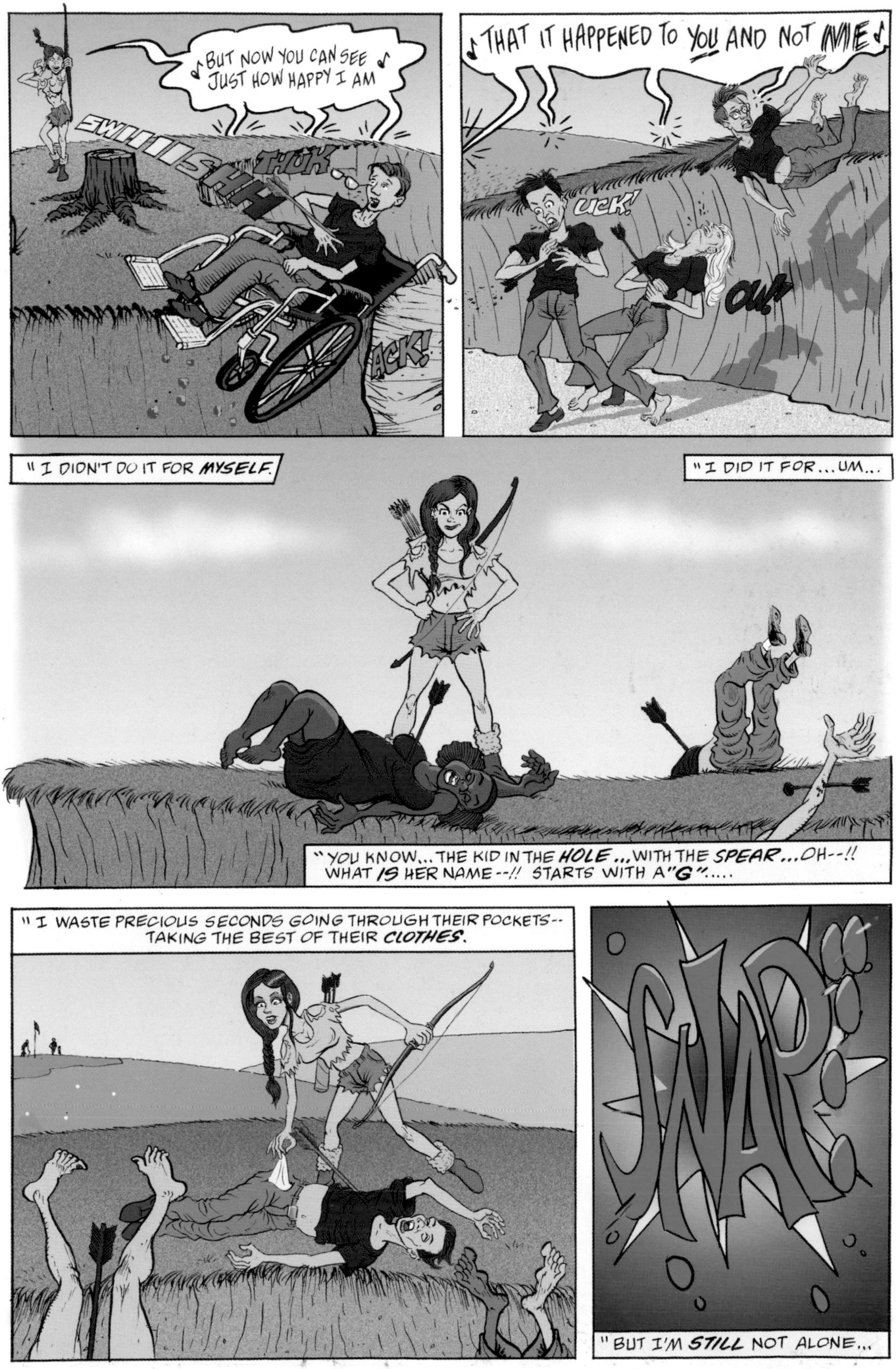
BUT NOW YOU CAN SEE JUST HOW HAPPY I AM
SWIIIISHH
THUK
ACK!
THAT IT HAPPENED TO YOU AND NOT ME
UCK!
OW!
" I DIDN'T DO IT FOR MYSELF.
" I DID IT FOR... UM...
" YOU KNOW... THE KID IN THE HOLE... WITH THE SPEAR... OH--!! WHAT IS HER NAME--!! STARTS WITH A "G"....
" I WASTE PRECIOUS SECONDS GOING THROUGH THEIR POCKETS-- TAKING THE BEST OF THEIR CLOTHES.
SNAP!
" BUT I'M STILL NOT ALONE...

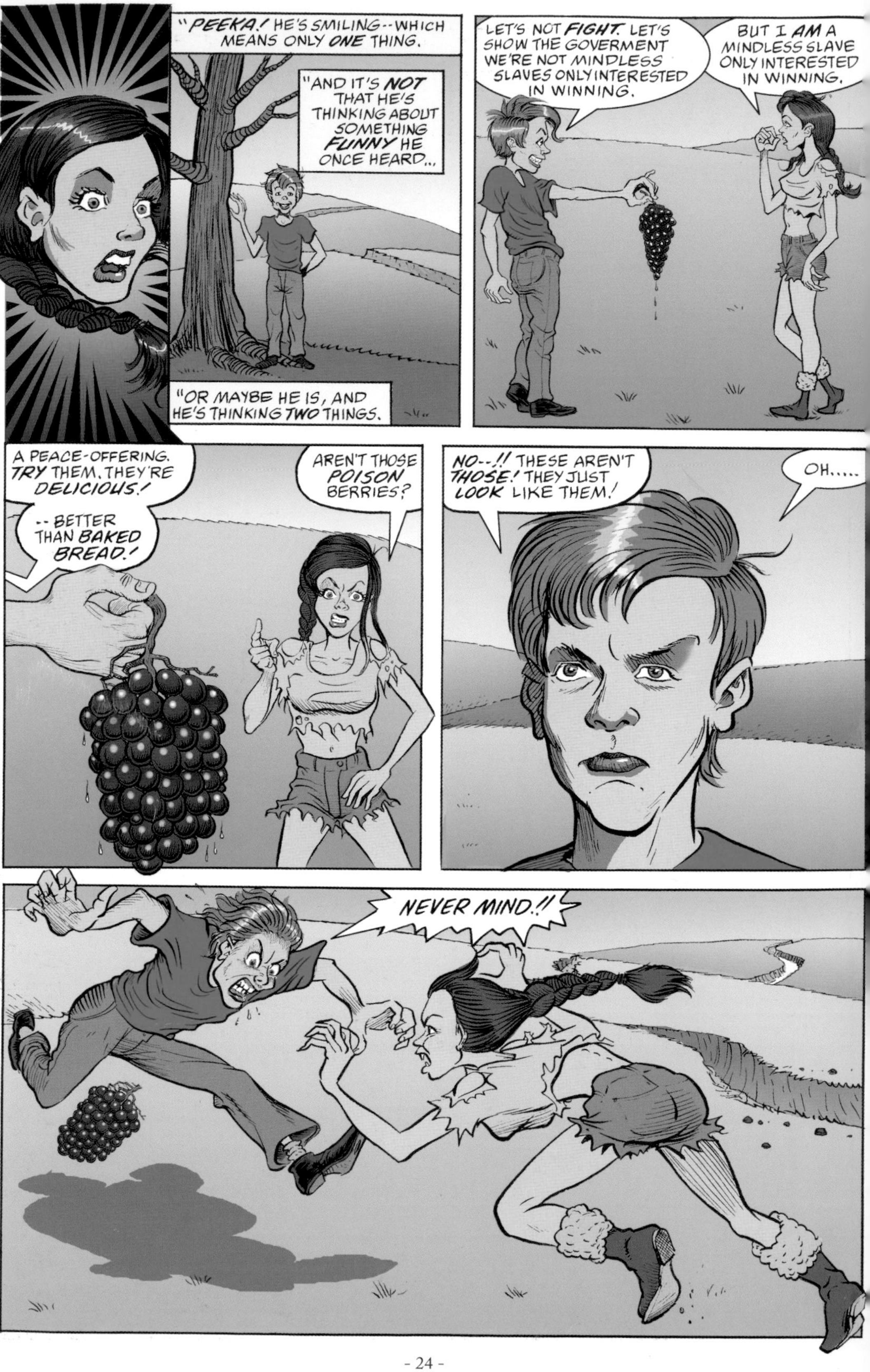
"PEEKA! HE'S SMILING--WHICH MEANS ONLY ONE THING.
"AND IT'S NOT THAT HE'S THINKING ABOUT SOMETHING FUNNY HE ONCE HEARD...
"OR MAYBE HE IS, AND HE'S THINKING TWO THINGS.
LET'S NOT FIGHT. LET'S SHOW THE GOVERMENT WE'RE NOT MINDLESS SLAVES ONLY INTERESTED IN WINNING.
BUT I AM A MINDLESS SLAVE ONLY INTERESTED IN WINNING.
A PEACE-OFFERING. TRY THEM. THEY'RE DELICIOUS!
--BETTER THAN BAKED BREAD!
AREN'T THOSE POISON BERRIES?
NO--!! THESE AREN'T THOSE! THEY JUST LOOK LIKE THEM!
OH.....
NEVER MIND!!

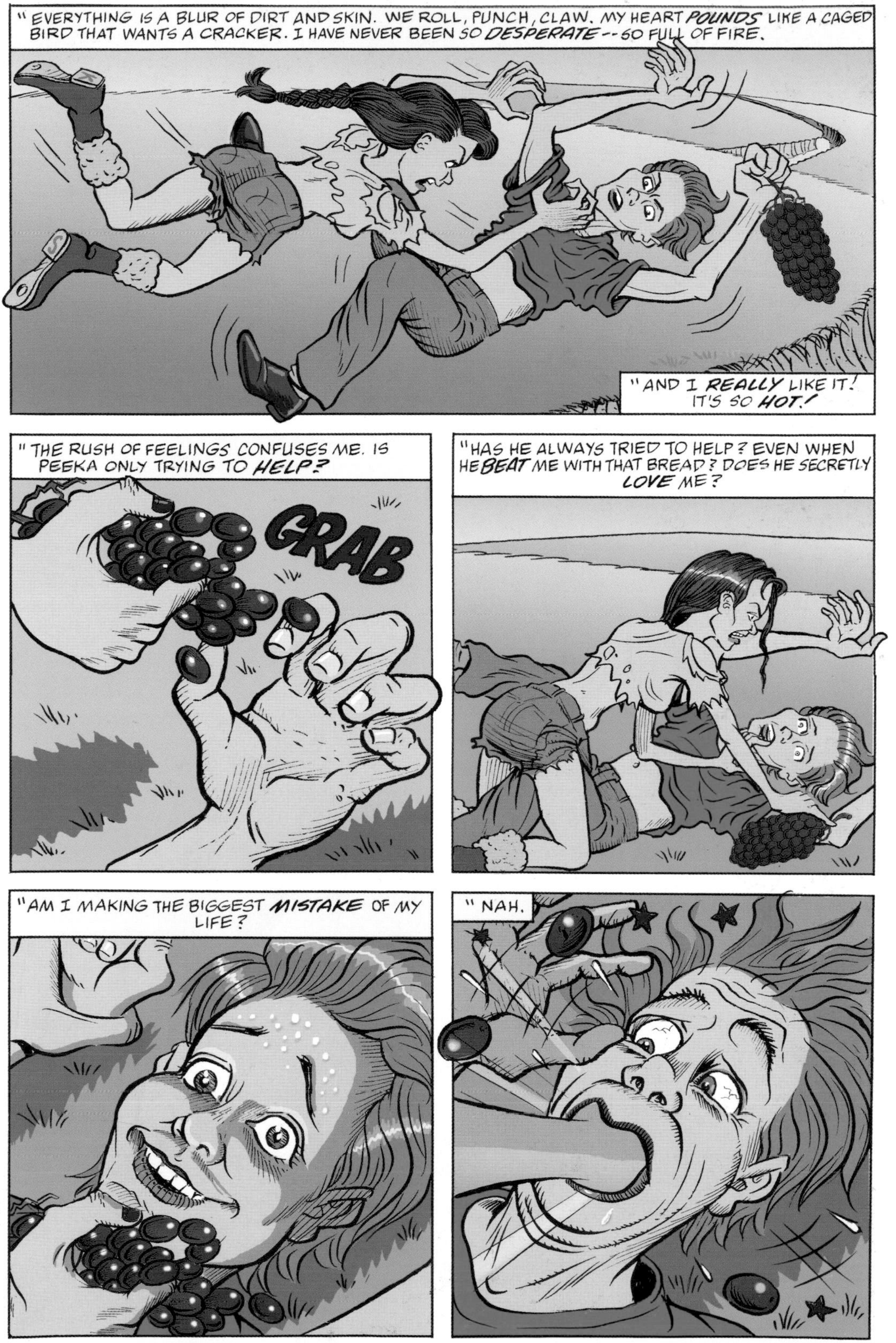
"EVERYTHING IS A BLUR OF DIRT AND SKIN. WE ROLL, PUNCH, CLAW. MY HEART POUNDS LIKE A CAGED BIRD THAT WANTS A CRACKER. I HAVE NEVER BEEN SO DESPERATE -- SO FULL OF FIRE.
"AND I REALLY LIKE IT! IT'S SO HOT!
"THE RUSH OF FEELINGS CONFUSES ME. IS PEEKA ONLY TRYING TO HELP?
GRAB
"HAS HE ALWAYS TRIED TO HELP? EVEN WHEN HE BEAT ME WITH THAT BREAD? DOES HE SECRETLY LOVE ME?
"AM I MAKING THE BIGGEST MISTAKE OF MY LIFE?
"NAH.

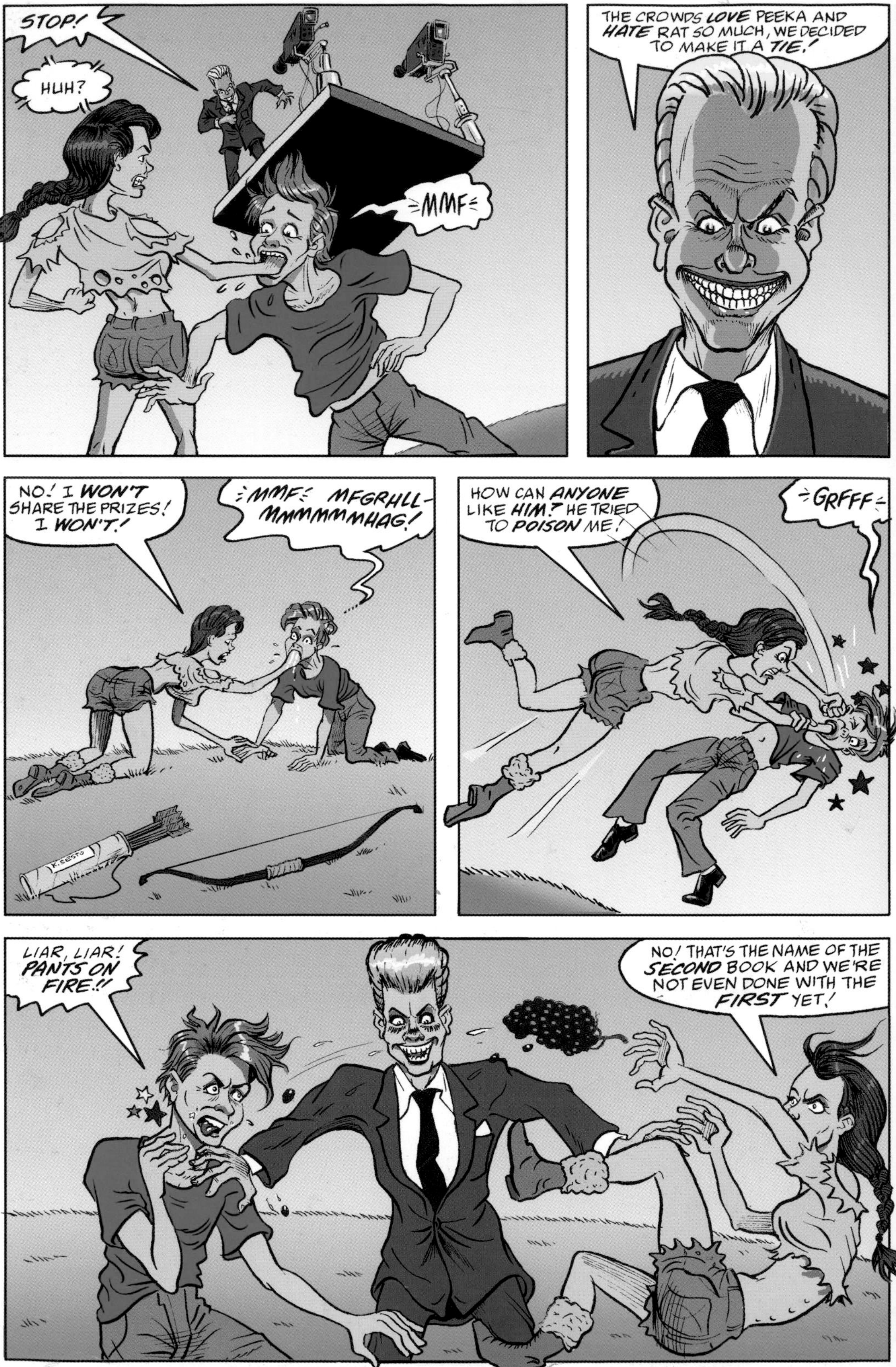
STOP!
HUH?
-MMF-
THE CROWDS LOVE PEEKA AND HATE RAT SO MUCH, WE DECIDED TO MAKE IT A TIE!
NO! I WON'T SHARE THE PRIZES! I WON'T!
-MMF- MFGRHLL-MMMMMMHAG!
K.SESTO
HOW CAN ANYONE LIKE HIM? HE TRIED TO POISON ME!
-GRFFF-
LIAR, LIAR! PANTS ON FIRE!!
NO! THAT'S THE NAME OF THE SECOND BOOK AND WE'RE NOT EVEN DONE WITH THE FIRST YET!

"DESPITE MY DISAPPOINTMENT, THINGS GET *BETTER* AFTER THE GAME.

"WE HAVE MORE *FAKE FOOD* THAN WE CAN EAT. BUT EVEN THAT WON'T KEEP DIM QUIET.

Y'THINK THERE'S AN *AFTERLIFE,* RAT? SO--IF I *DIED,* I'D SEE HOW SAD YOU WERE?

WOULDN'T THAT BE EVEN *SADDER?*

"I SHOULD HAVE KNOWN IT WOULDN'T LAST.

KNOK

KNOK
KNOK

"BUT EVEN *I* COULDN'T HAVE GUESSED WHO IT WAS. THAT'S WHAT MAKES THIS SO *EXCITING,* RIGHT?

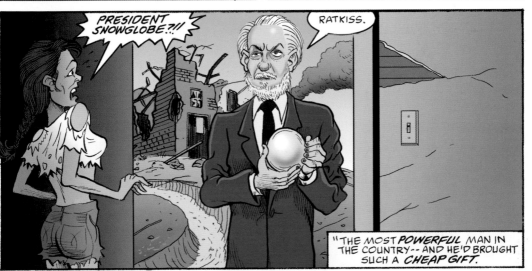

PRESIDENT SNOWGLOBE?!!

RATKISS.

"THE MOST *POWERFUL* MAN IN THE COUNTRY-- AND HE'D BROUGHT SUCH A *CHEAP GIFT.*

KICK ME

SNIF

IS THAT THE SMELL OF *BLOOD* AND *ROSES* THEY SAY YOU ALWAYS EXUDE FROM INGESTING THE *POISON* YOU USE ON YOUR *ENEMIES?*

MAIL

NO, I *FARTED.*

MAY I COME STRAIGHT TO THE *POINT?*

I THINK YOU ALREADY *HAVE.*

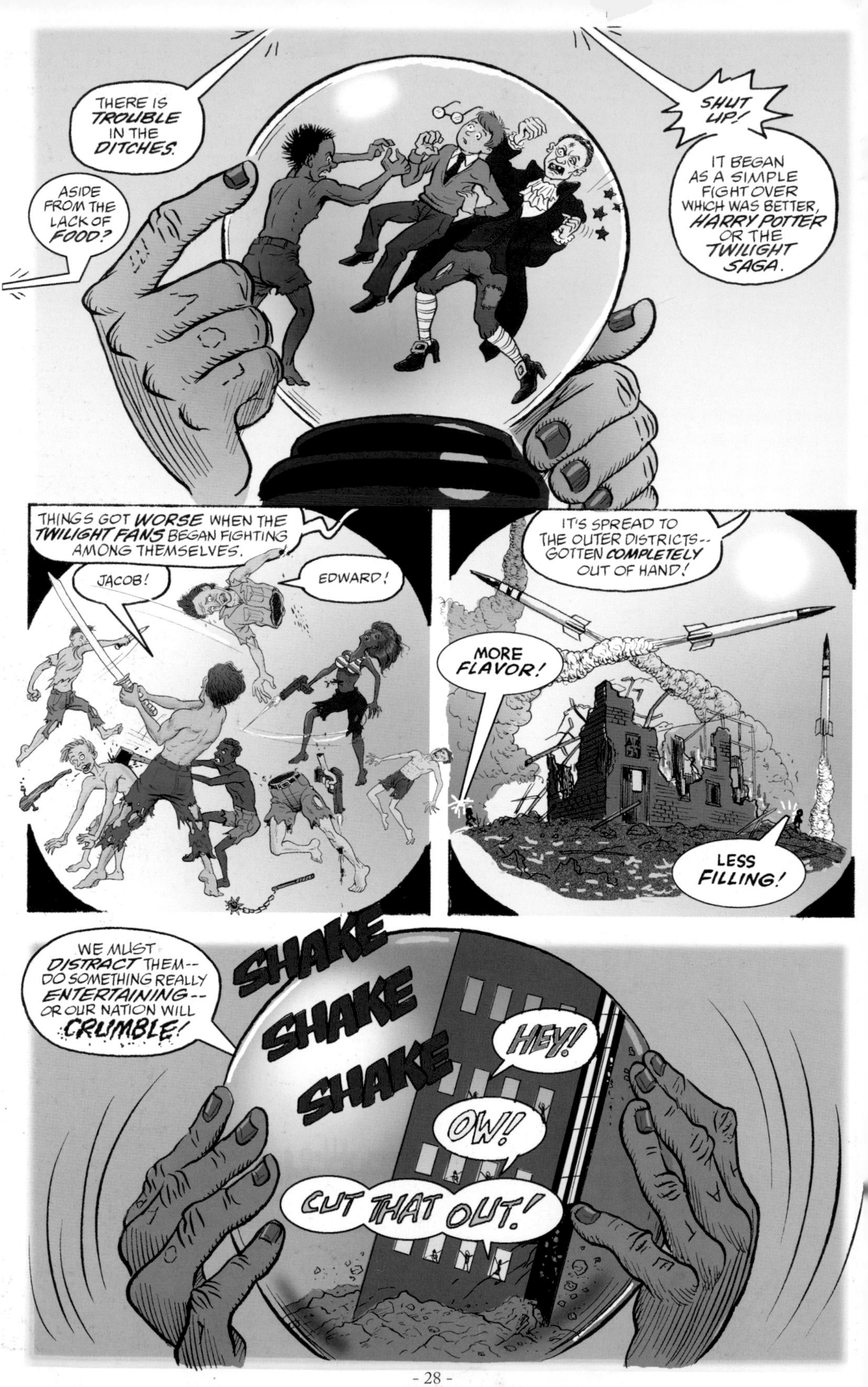
THERE IS TROUBLE IN THE DITCHES.
ASIDE FROM THE LACK OF FOOD?
SHUT UP!
IT BEGAN AS A SIMPLE FIGHT OVER WHICH WAS BETTER, HARRY POTTER OR THE TWILIGHT SAGA.
THINGS GOT WORSE WHEN THE TWILIGHT FANS BEGAN FIGHTING AMONG THEMSELVES.
JACOB!
EDWARD!
IT'S SPREAD TO THE OUTER DISTRICTS-- GOTTEN COMPLETELY OUT OF HAND!
MORE FLAVOR!
LESS FILLING!
WE MUST DISTRACT THEM-- DO SOMETHING REALLY ENTERTAINING-- OR OUR NATION WILL CRUMBLE!
SHAKE
SHAKE
SHAKE
HEY!
OW!
CUT THAT OUT!

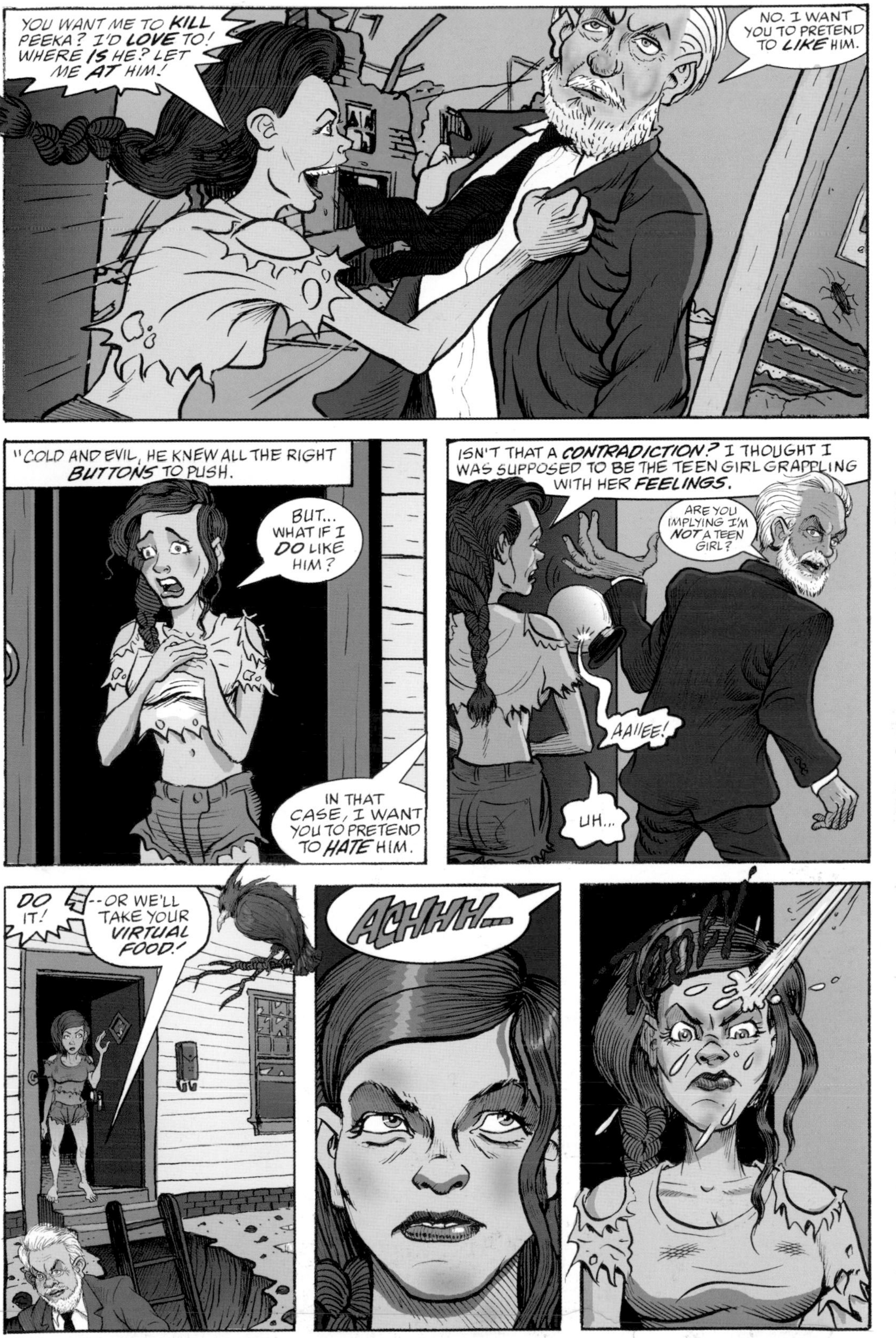
YOU WANT ME TO KILL PEEKA? I'D LOVE TO! WHERE IS HE? LET ME AT HIM!
NO. I WANT YOU TO PRETEND TO LIKE HIM.
"COLD AND EVIL, HE KNEW ALL THE RIGHT BUTTONS TO PUSH.
BUT... WHAT IF I DO LIKE HIM?
IN THAT CASE, I WANT YOU TO PRETEND TO HATE HIM.
ISN'T THAT A CONTRADICTION? I THOUGHT I WAS SUPPOSED TO BE THE TEEN GIRL GRAPPLING WITH HER FEELINGS.
ARE YOU IMPLYING I'M NOT A TEEN GIRL?
AAIIEE!
UH...
DO IT!
--OR WE'LL TAKE YOUR VIRTUAL FOOD!
ACHHH...

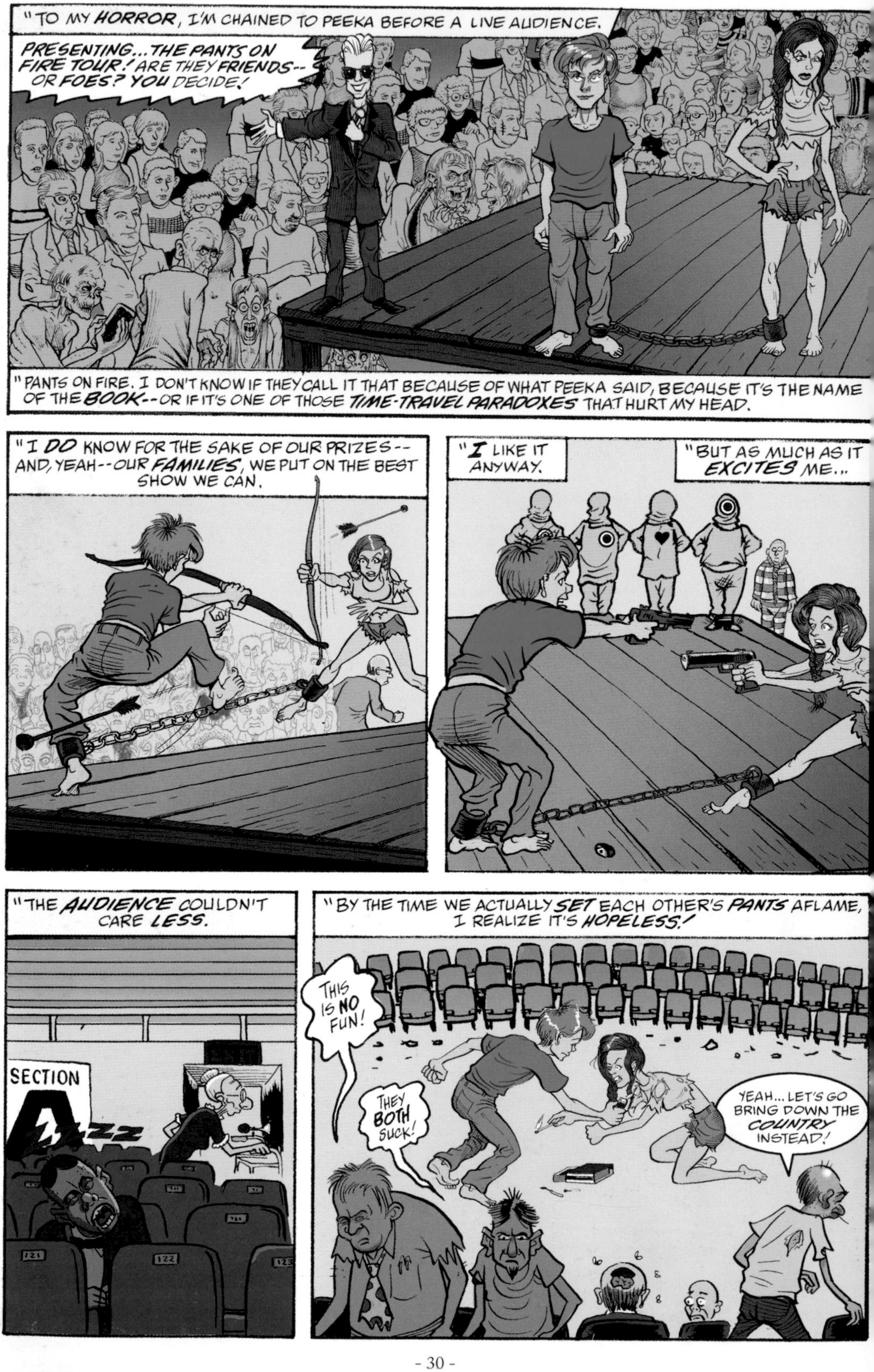
"TO MY HORROR, I'M CHAINED TO PEEKA BEFORE A LIVE AUDIENCE.
PRESENTING... THE PANTS ON FIRE TOUR! ARE THEY FRIENDS-- OR FOES? YOU DECIDE!
"PANTS ON FIRE. I DON'T KNOW IF THEY CALL IT THAT BECAUSE OF WHAT PEEKA SAID, BECAUSE IT'S THE NAME OF THE BOOK--OR IF IT'S ONE OF THOSE TIME-TRAVEL PARADOXES THAT HURT MY HEAD.
"I DO KNOW FOR THE SAKE OF OUR PRIZES-- AND, YEAH--OUR FAMILIES, WE PUT ON THE BEST SHOW WE CAN.
"I LIKE IT ANYWAY.
"BUT AS MUCH AS IT EXCITES ME...
"THE AUDIENCE COULDN'T CARE LESS.
SECTION
A
ZZZ
"BY THE TIME WE ACTUALLY SET EACH OTHER'S PANTS AFLAME, I REALIZE IT'S HOPELESS!
THIS IS NO FUN!
THEY BOTH SUCK!
YEAH... LET'S GO BRING DOWN THE COUNTRY INSTEAD!

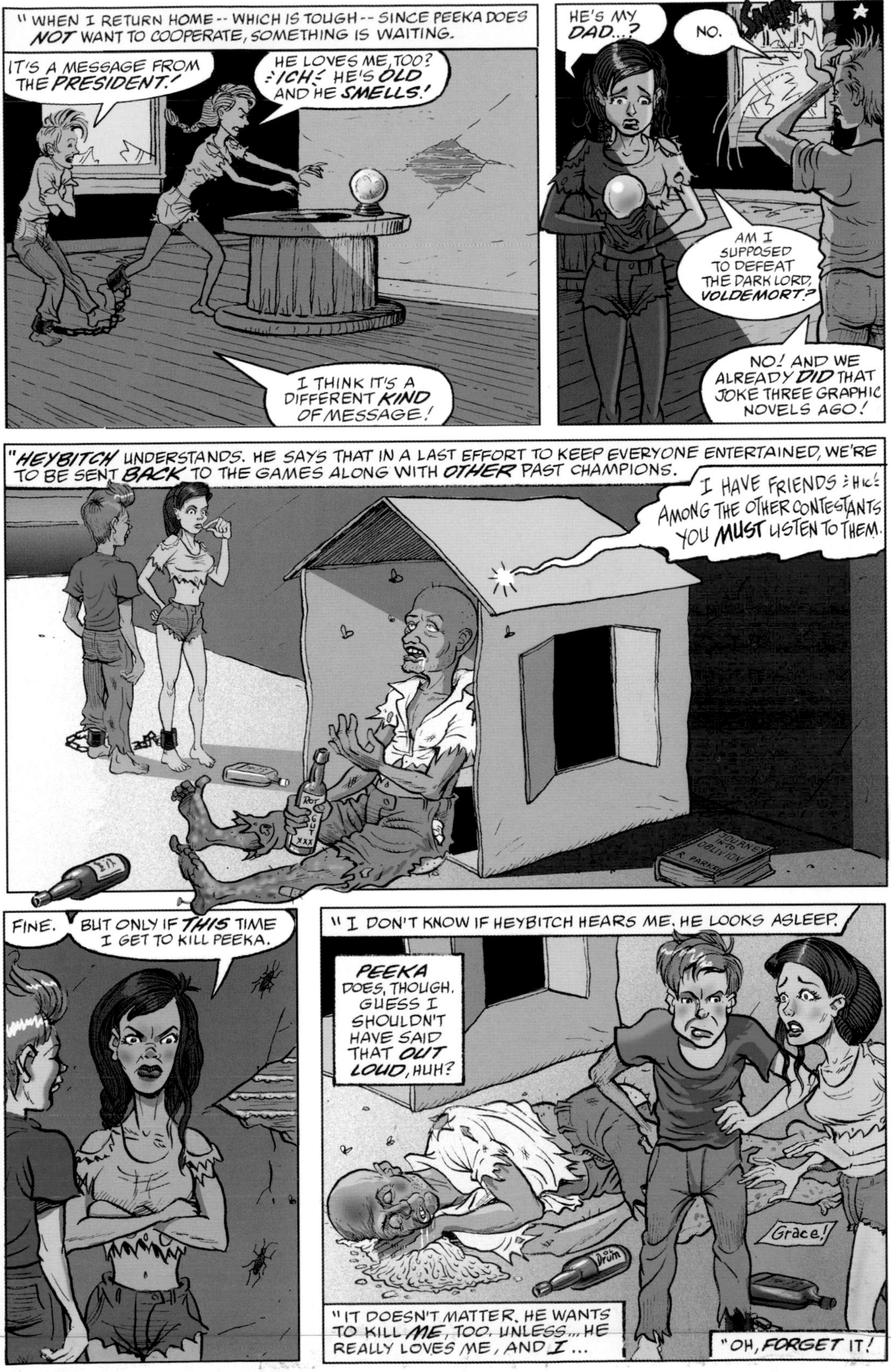
"WHEN I RETURN HOME -- WHICH IS TOUGH -- SINCE PEEKA DOES NOT WANT TO COOPERATE, SOMETHING IS WAITING.
IT'S A MESSAGE FROM THE PRESIDENT!
HE LOVES ME, TOO? ICH! HE'S OLD AND HE SMELLS!
I THINK IT'S A DIFFERENT KIND OF MESSAGE!
HE'S MY DAD...?
NO.
AM I SUPPOSED TO DEFEAT THE DARK LORD, VOLDEMORT?
NO! AND WE ALREADY DID THAT JOKE THREE GRAPHIC NOVELS AGO!
"HEYBITCH UNDERSTANDS. HE SAYS THAT IN A LAST EFFORT TO KEEP EVERYONE ENTERTAINED, WE'RE TO BE SENT BACK TO THE GAMES ALONG WITH OTHER PAST CHAMPIONS.
I HAVE FRIENDS HIC! AMONG THE OTHER CONTESTANTS YOU MUST LISTEN TO THEM.
ROT GUT XXX
JOURNEY INTO OBLIVION R. PARKER
FINE.
BUT ONLY IF THIS TIME I GET TO KILL PEEKA.
"I DON'T KNOW IF HEYBITCH HEARS ME. HE LOOKS ASLEEP.
PEEKA DOES, THOUGH. GUESS I SHOULDN'T HAVE SAID THAT OUT LOUD, HUH?
Grace!
"IT DOESN'T MATTER. HE WANTS TO KILL ME, TOO. UNLESS... HE REALLY LOVES ME, AND I ...
"OH, FORGET IT!

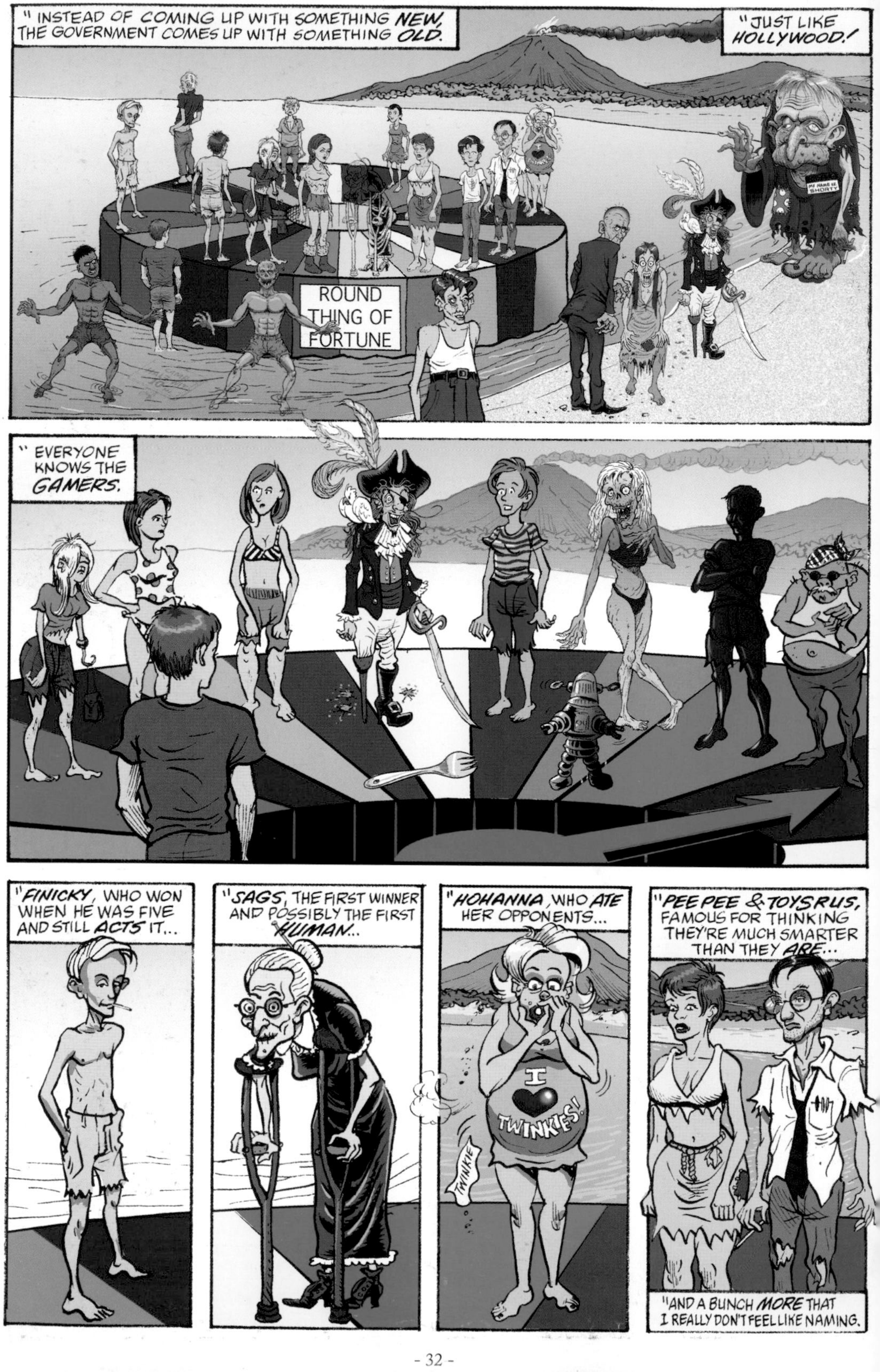
"INSTEAD OF COMING UP WITH SOMETHING NEW, THE GOVERNMENT COMES UP WITH SOMETHING OLD.
"JUST LIKE HOLLYWOOD!
ROUND THING OF FORTUNE
MY NAME IS SHORTY
"EVERYONE KNOWS THE GAMERS.
"FINICKY, WHO WON WHEN HE WAS FIVE AND STILL ACTS IT...
"SAGS, THE FIRST WINNER AND POSSIBLY THE FIRST HUMAN...
"HOHANNA, WHO ATE HER OPPONENTS...
I ♥ TWINKIES!
TWINKIE
"PEE PEE & TOYSRUS, FAMOUS FOR THINKING THEY'RE MUCH SMARTER THAN THEY ARE...
"AND A BUNCH MORE THAT I REALLY DON'T FEEL LIKE NAMING.

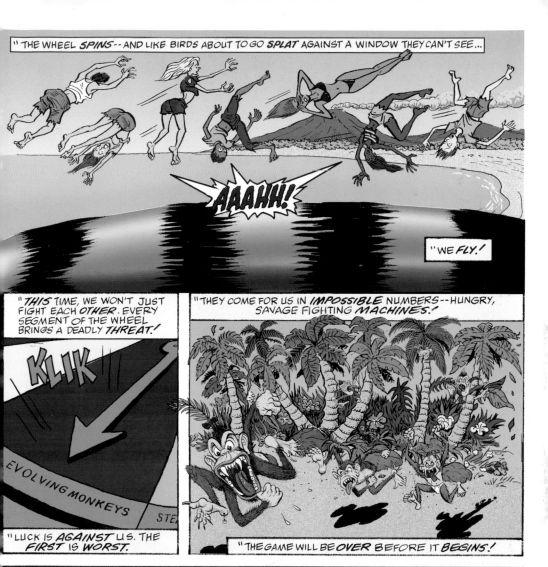

" THE WHEEL *SPINS*-- AND LIKE BIRDS ABOUT TO GO *SPLAT* AGAINST A WINDOW THEY CAN'T SEE...

AAAHH!

"WE *FLY!*

"*THIS* TIME, WE WON'T JUST FIGHT EACH *OTHER*. EVERY SEGMENT OF THE WHEEL BRINGS A DEADLY *THREAT!*

KLIK

EVOLVING MONKEYS

STE

"LUCK IS *AGAINST* US. THE *FIRST* IS *WORST*.

"THEY COME FOR US IN *IMPOSSIBLE* NUMBERS--HUNGRY, SAVAGE FIGHTING *MACHINES!*

"THE GAME WILL BE *OVER* BEFORE IT *BEGINS!*

" I DON'T GIVE UP--! I CAN'T.!!

''NOT WITH ALL THOSE *PRIZES* WAITING BACK HOME...,

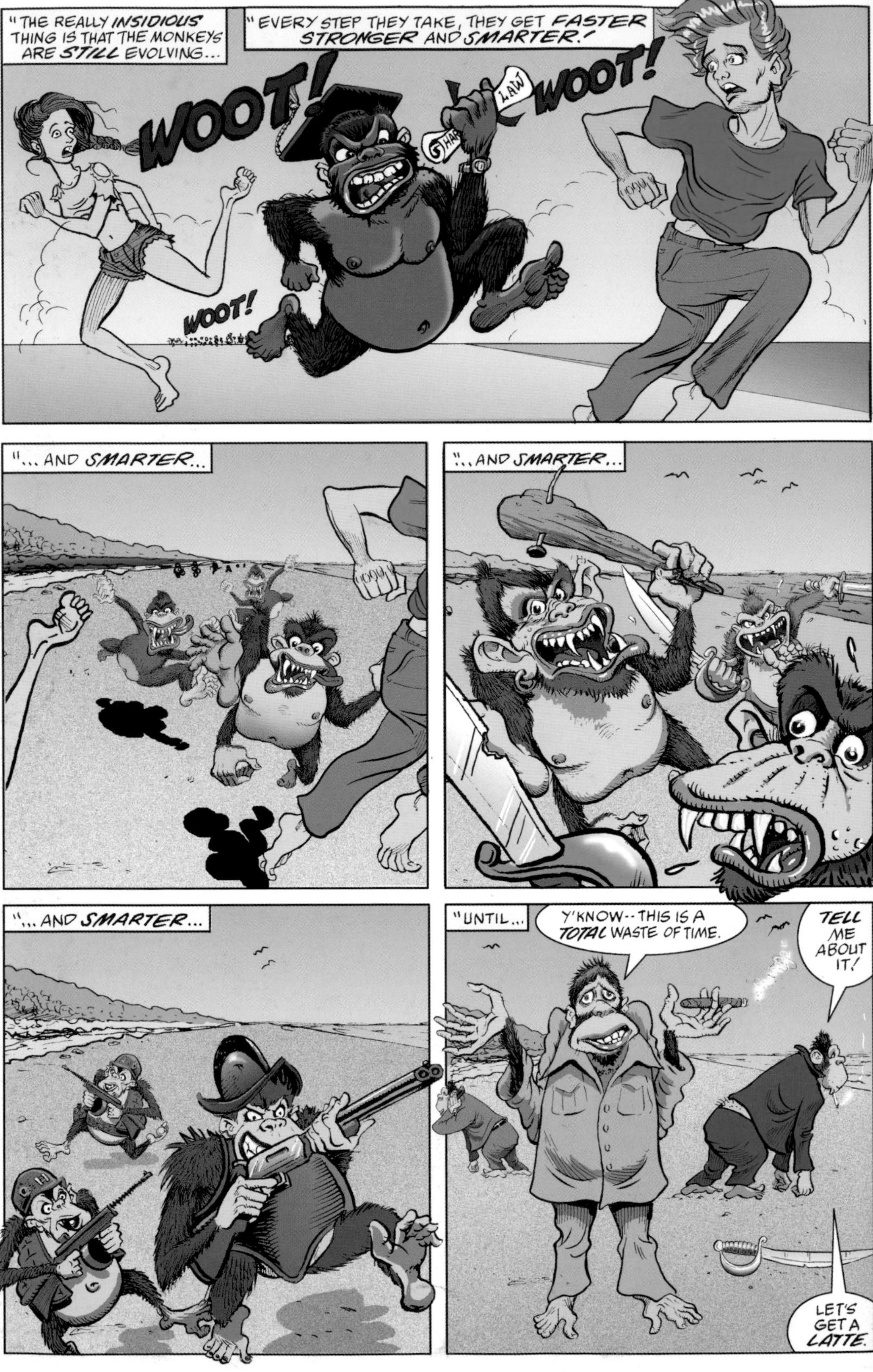
"THE REALLY INSIDIOUS THING IS THAT THE MONKEYS ARE STILL EVOLVING...
"EVERY STEP THEY TAKE, THEY GET FASTER STRONGER AND SMARTER.'
WOOT!
LAW
WOOT!
WOOT!
"... AND SMARTER...
"... AND SMARTER...
"... AND SMARTER...
"UNTIL...
Y'KNOW-- THIS IS A TOTAL WASTE OF TIME.
TELL ME ABOUT IT!
LET'S GET A LATTE.

"AS THE APES CARVE iPHONES FROM TREE BARK, IT DAWNS ON ME WE'RE STILL *ALIVE*. EXCEPT MAYBE *SAGS*.

"THERE'S *PEEKA*-- PART OF MY LIFE, AS HE'S ALWAYS BEEN.

MUNCH CRUNCH

PANT! PANT!

WHAT DO I FEEL FOR HIM? *HATE*? *LOVE*?

"OR SOMETHING I CAN'T EVEN PRONOUNCE-- LIKE *AJSHFHGREU*?

"MAYBE I'LL FIND OUT AFTER I *KILL HIM*.

?

"LIKE THE SONG SAYS, BETTER *HIM* THAN *ME*.

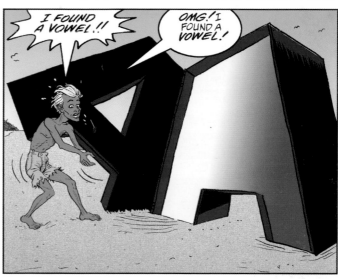

I FOUND A *VOWEL*!!

OMG! I FOUND A *VOWEL!*

"I FEEL *HANDS* ON ME, RUINING MY *SHOT*, DRAGGING ME...

TWINKIE

...*WHERE?*

!

THUK

"ALL AT ONCE, I REALIZE HEYBITCH'S *PLAN*...

"THE STUPID DRUNK MADE *ME* PART OF AN *ESCAPE!*

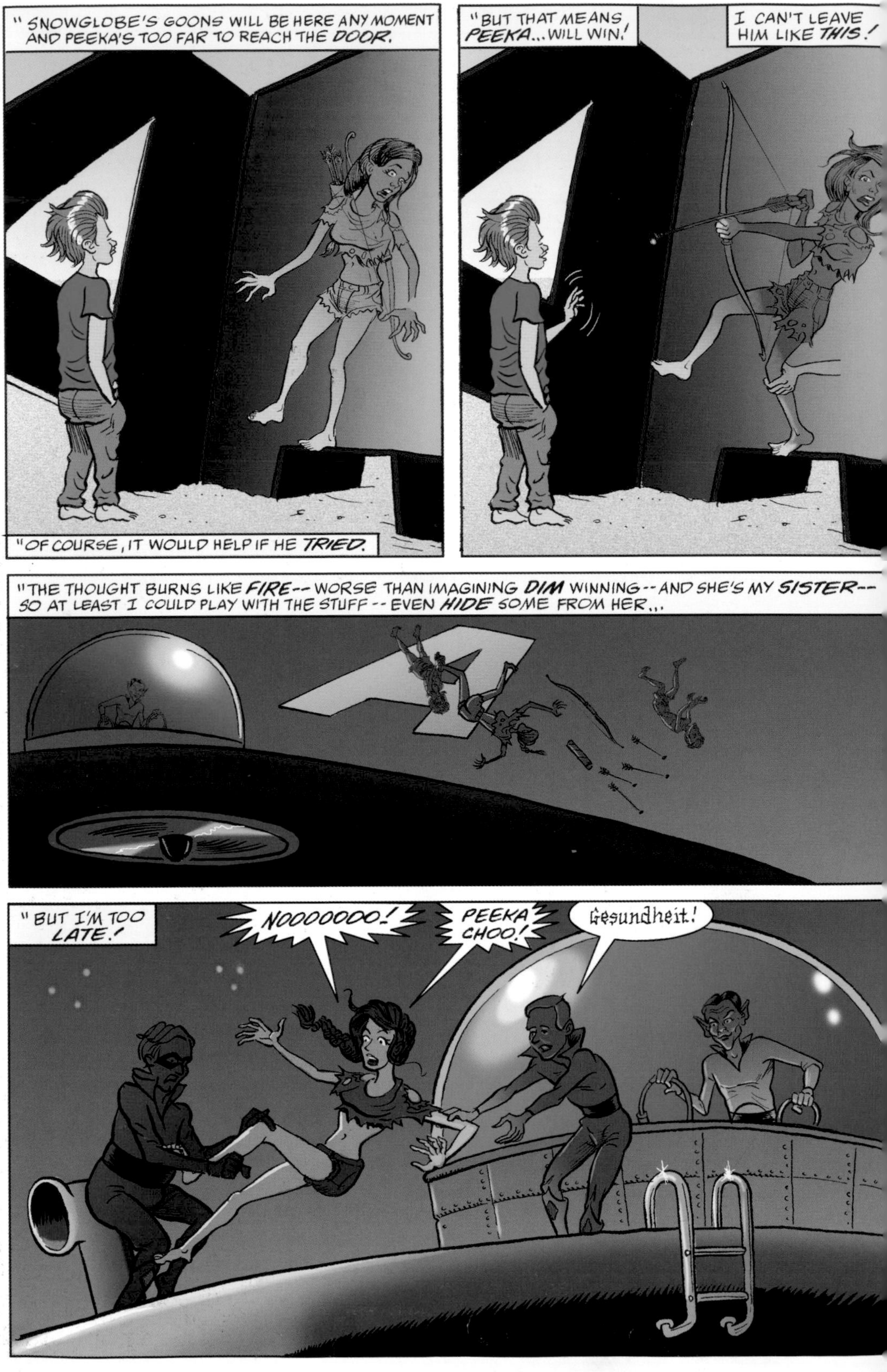
"SNOWGLOBE'S GOONS WILL BE HERE ANY MOMENT AND PEEKA'S TOO FAR TO REACH THE DOOR.
"OF COURSE, IT WOULD HELP IF HE TRIED.
"BUT THAT MEANS PEEKA... WILL WIN.'
I CAN'T LEAVE HIM LIKE THIS!
"THE THOUGHT BURNS LIKE FIRE-- WORSE THAN IMAGINING DIM WINNING-- AND SHE'S MY SISTER-- SO AT LEAST I COULD PLAY WITH THE STUFF-- EVEN HIDE SOME FROM HER...
"BUT I'M TOO LATE.'
NOOOOOOO!
PEEKA CHOO!
Gesundheit!

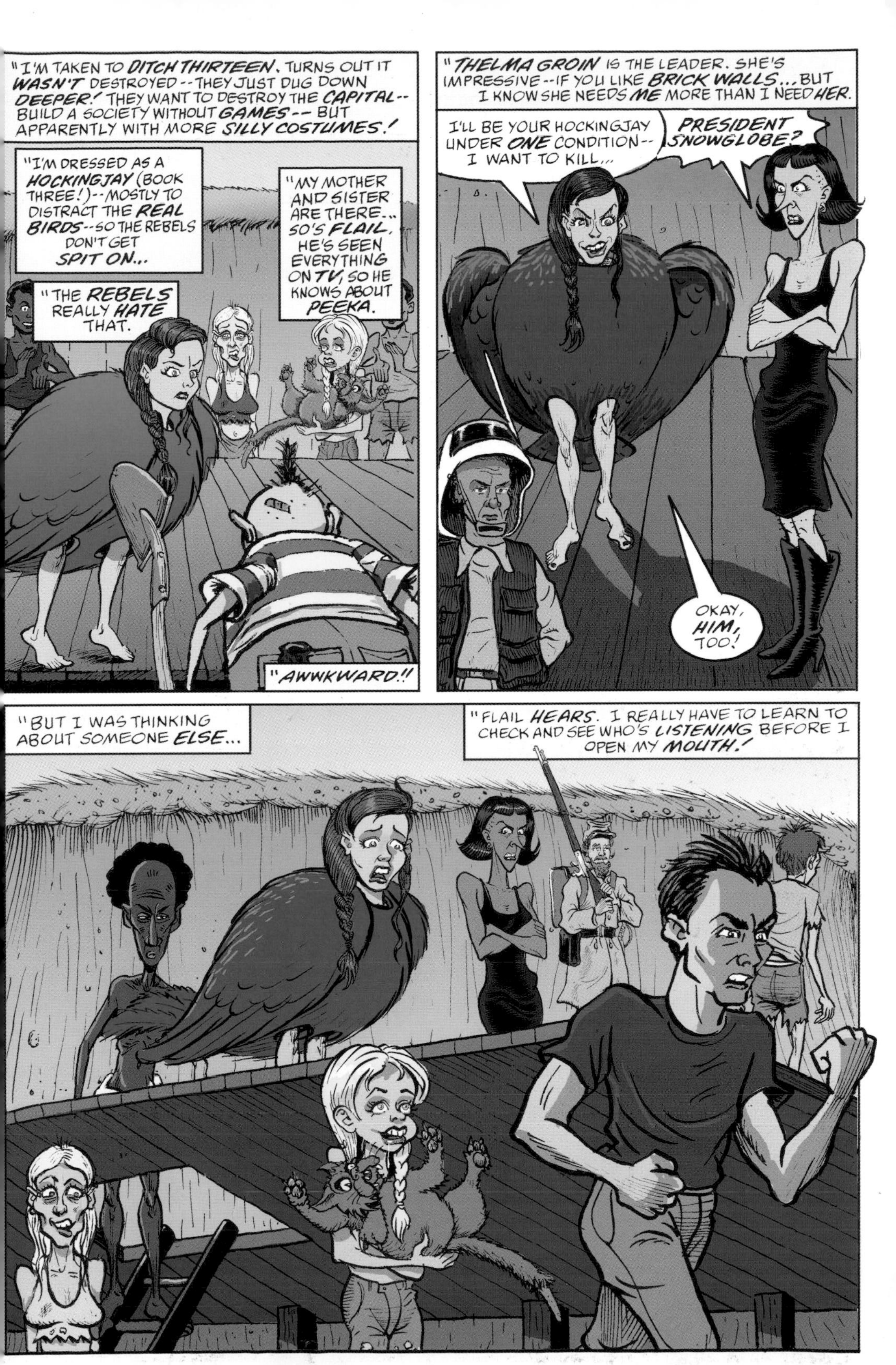
"I'M TAKEN TO DITCH THIRTEEN. TURNS OUT IT WASN'T DESTROYED--THEY JUST DUG DOWN DEEPER! THEY WANT TO DESTROY THE CAPITAL--BUILD A SOCIETY WITHOUT GAMES--BUT APPARENTLY WITH MORE SILLY COSTUMES!
"I'M DRESSED AS A HOCKINGJAY (BOOK THREE!)--MOSTLY TO DISTRACT THE REAL BIRDS--SO THE REBELS DON'T GET SPIT ON...
"MY MOTHER AND SISTER ARE THERE... SO'S FLAIL. HE'S SEEN EVERYTHING ON TV, SO HE KNOWS ABOUT PEEKA.
"THE REBELS REALLY HATE THAT.
"AWWKWARD!!
"THELMA GROIN IS THE LEADER. SHE'S IMPRESSIVE--IF YOU LIKE BRICK WALLS... BUT I KNOW SHE NEEDS ME MORE THAN I NEED HER.
I'LL BE YOUR HOCKINGJAY UNDER ONE CONDITION--I WANT TO KILL...
PRESIDENT SNOWGLOBE?
OKAY, HIM, TOO!
"BUT I WAS THINKING ABOUT SOMEONE ELSE...
"FLAIL HEARS. I REALLY HAVE TO LEARN TO CHECK AND SEE WHO'S LISTENING BEFORE I OPEN MY MOUTH!

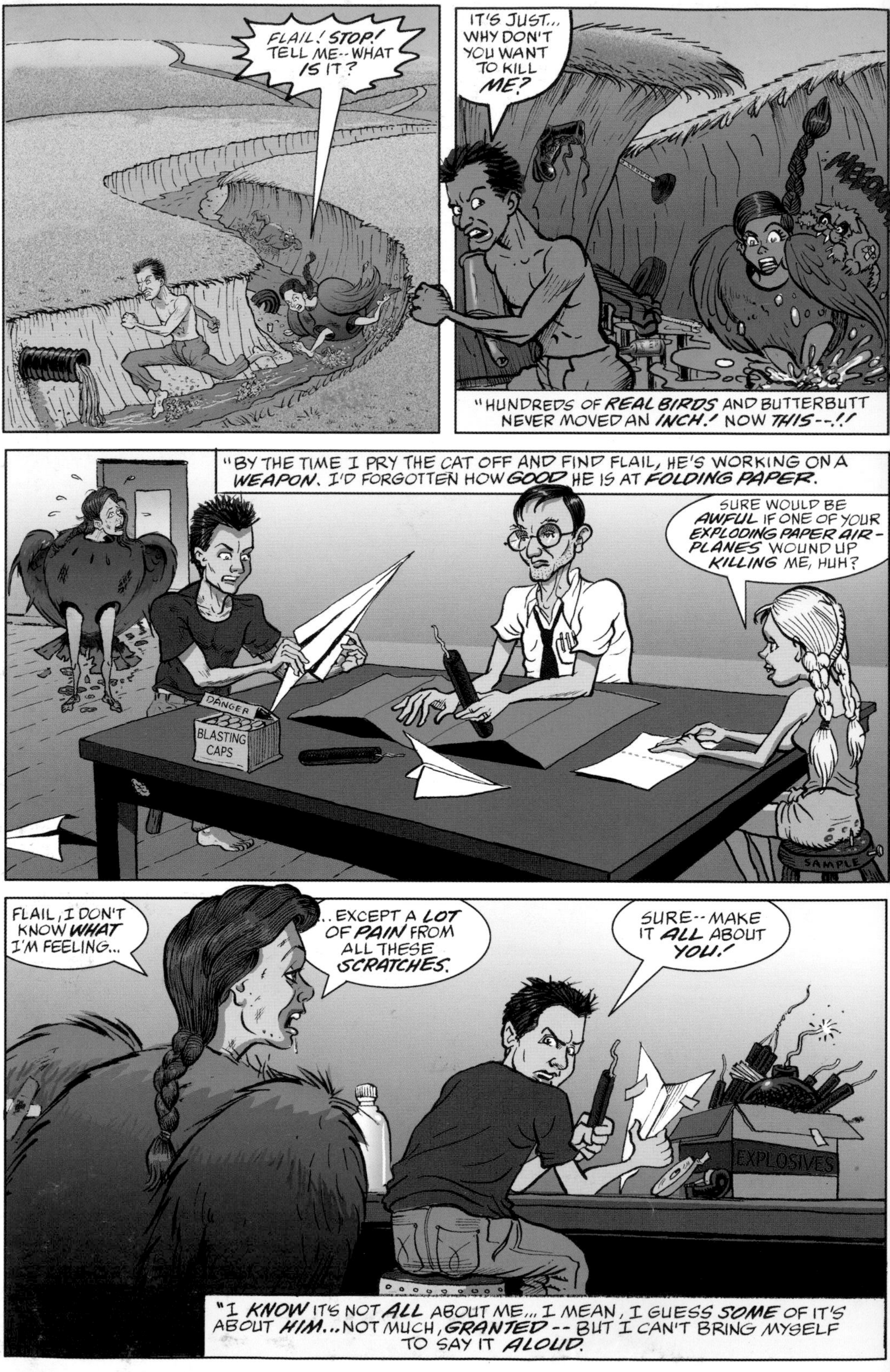
FLAIL! STOP! TELL ME--WHAT IS IT?
IT'S JUST... WHY DON'T YOU WANT TO KILL ME?
"HUNDREDS OF REAL BIRDS AND BUTTERBUTT NEVER MOVED AN INCH! NOW THIS--!!
"BY THE TIME I PRY THE CAT OFF AND FIND FLAIL, HE'S WORKING ON A WEAPON. I'D FORGOTTEN HOW GOOD HE IS AT FOLDING PAPER.
SURE WOULD BE AWFUL IF ONE OF YOUR EXPLODING PAPER AIR-PLANES WOUND UP KILLING ME, HUH?
DANGER
BLASTING CAPS
SAMPLE
FLAIL, I DON'T KNOW WHAT I'M FEELING...
...EXCEPT A LOT OF PAIN FROM ALL THESE SCRATCHES.
SURE--MAKE IT ALL ABOUT YOU!
EXPLOSIVES
"I KNOW IT'S NOT ALL ABOUT ME... I MEAN, I GUESS SOME OF IT'S ABOUT HIM...NOT MUCH, GRANTED -- BUT I CAN'T BRING MYSELF TO SAY IT ALOUD.

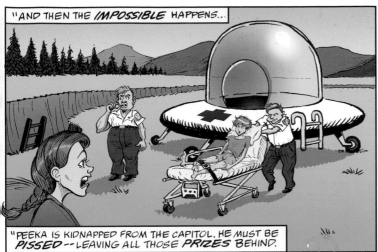

"AND THEN THE *IMPOSSIBLE* HAPPENS...

"PEEKA IS KIDNAPPED FROM THE CAPITOL. HE MUST BE *PISSED* -- LEAVING ALL THOSE *PRIZES* BEHIND.

"AS FOR *ME*, LOVE OR HATE, I'M *ITCHING* FOR A GOOD FIGHT. I DON'T EVEN WAIT UNTIL HE GETS *UP.*

"I KNOW IN AN *INSTANT* SOMETHING IS *WRONG.*

AIIEE!

"HE'S *CHANGED.*

AIEEE?

I... L♥VE YOU!

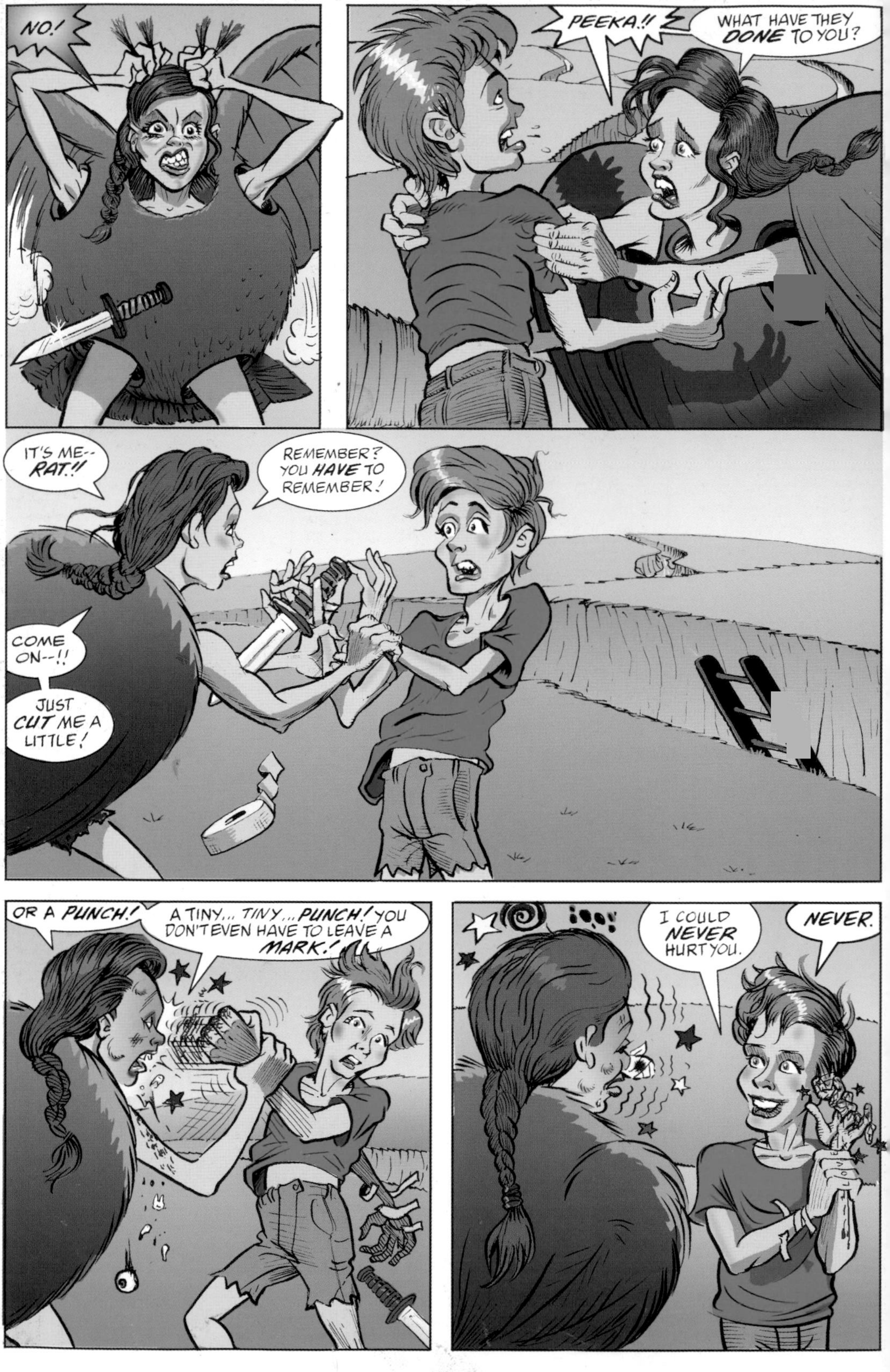
NO!
PEEKA!!
WHAT HAVE THEY DONE TO YOU?
IT'S ME-- RAT!!
REMEMBER? YOU HAVE TO REMEMBER!
COME ON--!!
JUST CUT ME A LITTLE!
OR A PUNCH!
A TINY... TINY... PUNCH! YOU DON'T EVEN HAVE TO LEAVE A MARK!
I COULD NEVER HURT YOU.
NEVER.

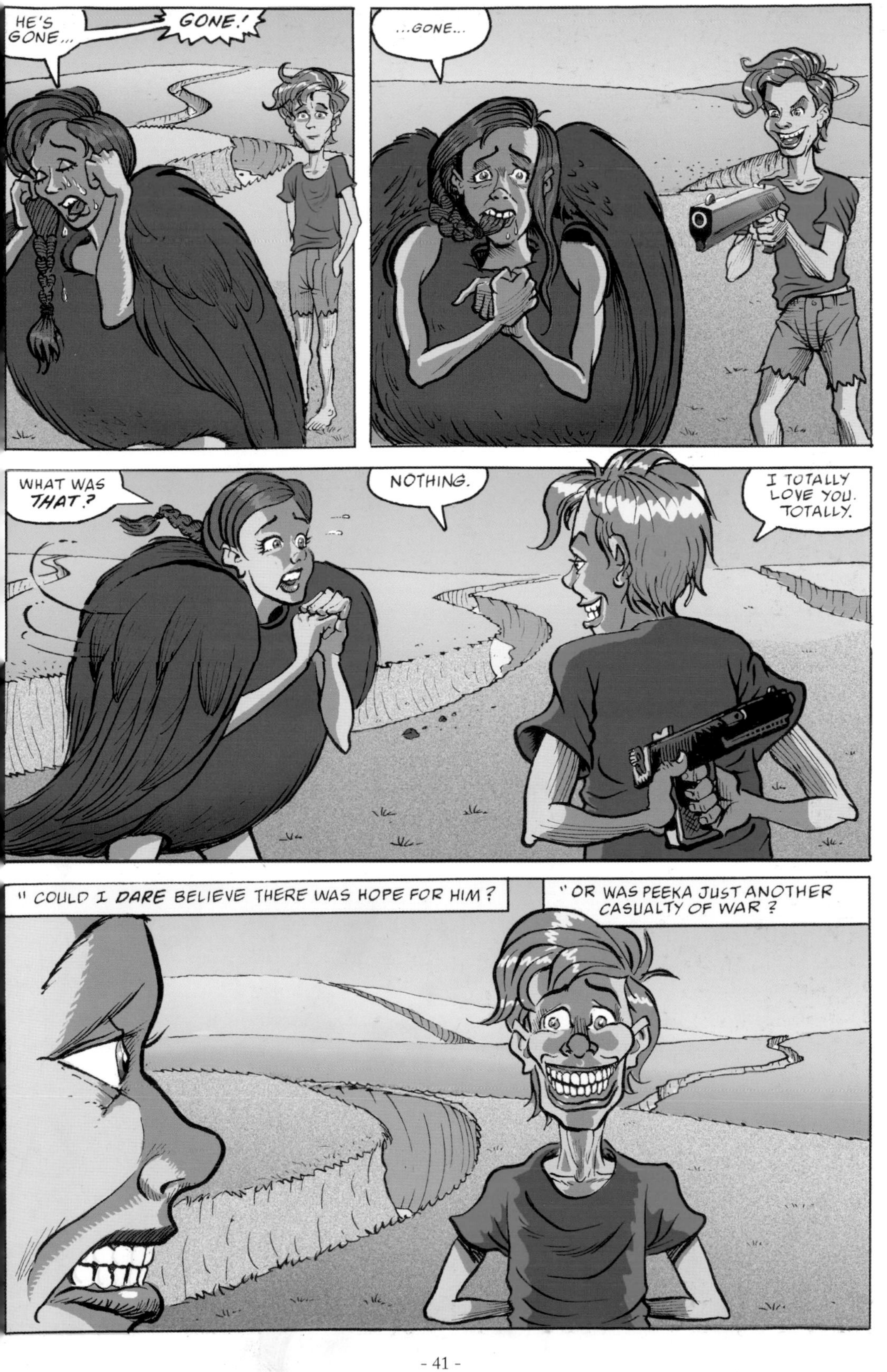
HE'S GONE...
GONE!
...GONE...
WHAT WAS THAT?
NOTHING.
I TOTALLY LOVE YOU. TOTALLY.
" COULD I DARE BELIEVE THERE WAS HOPE FOR HIM?
" OR WAS PEEKA JUST ANOTHER CASUALTY OF WAR?

"AS THE WAR DRAGS ON, THE *REBELS* WANT TO SEE THEIR *HOCKINGJAY*--SO THEY SEND A SMALL BAND OF US TO *BROADCAST* FROM A SUPPOSEDLY "SAFE" BATTLE.

BOOM

BACK UP...

...JUST A *LITTLE* MORE...

...*ONE* MORE STEP...

"BUT NOTHING IS SAFE IN *WAR*.

AAAH!

PERFECT!

"THAT'S WHY THEY CALL IT A *WAR*, AND NOT A *PEACE*-- OR SOMETHING ELSE-- LIKE A *CHAIR*.

"BUT CALLING IT *CHAIR* WOULD JUST BE *SILLY*.

OKAY...JUST A LITTLE MORE... *ONE* MORE STEP...

GOT IT!

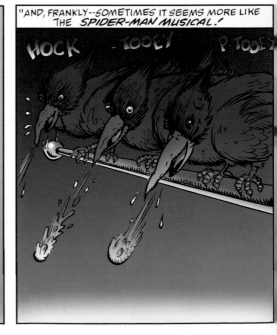

"AND, FRANKLY--SOMETIMES IT SEEMS MORE LIKE THE *SPIDER-MAN MUSICAL!*

HOCK - TOOEY   P.TOOEY

"SOON THE CAPITOL IS READY TO FALL -- BUT AT WHAT *COST?* IT SEEMS THE WORLD ITSELF HAS ALREADY *BEEN* DESTROYED.

"WE STAND FOR OUR *FINAL* BROADCAST SURROUNDED BY BROKEN BODIES AND *RUINS.*

"*DEATH* INFECTS THE VERY *AIR*-- FILLS OUR LUNGS-- COVERS OUR SKIN-- EMBEDS THE FABRIC OF OUR CLOTHES, --OUR *BEING.*

KLUNK

"*SMILE* EVERYONE!

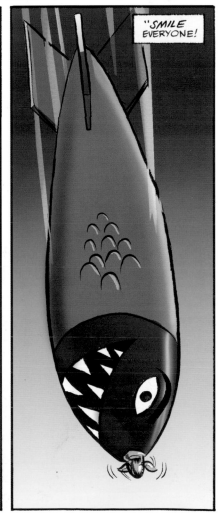

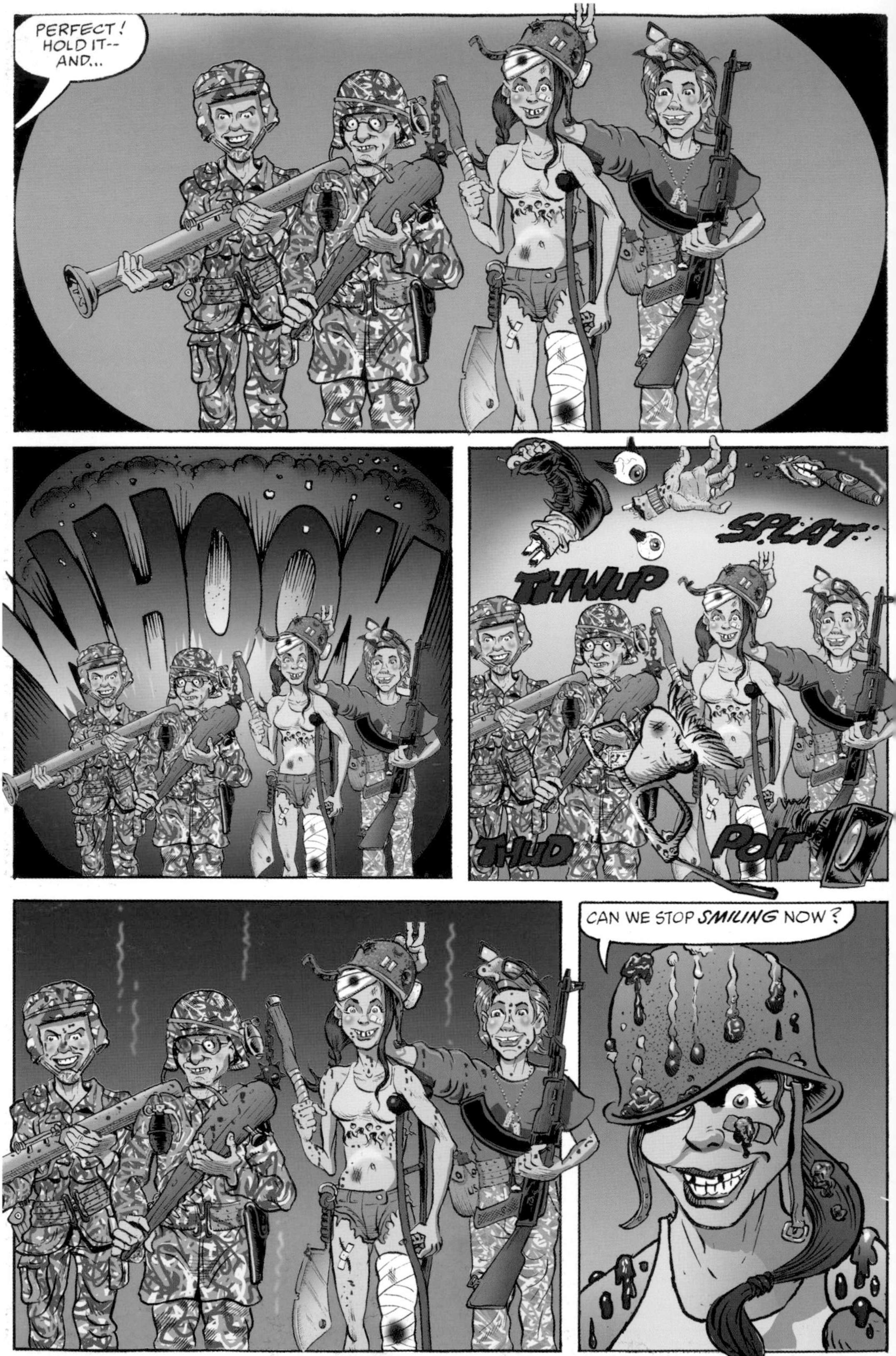
PERFECT! HOLD IT-- AND...
WHOOM
SPLAT
THWUP
THUD
POIT
CAN WE STOP SMILING NOW?

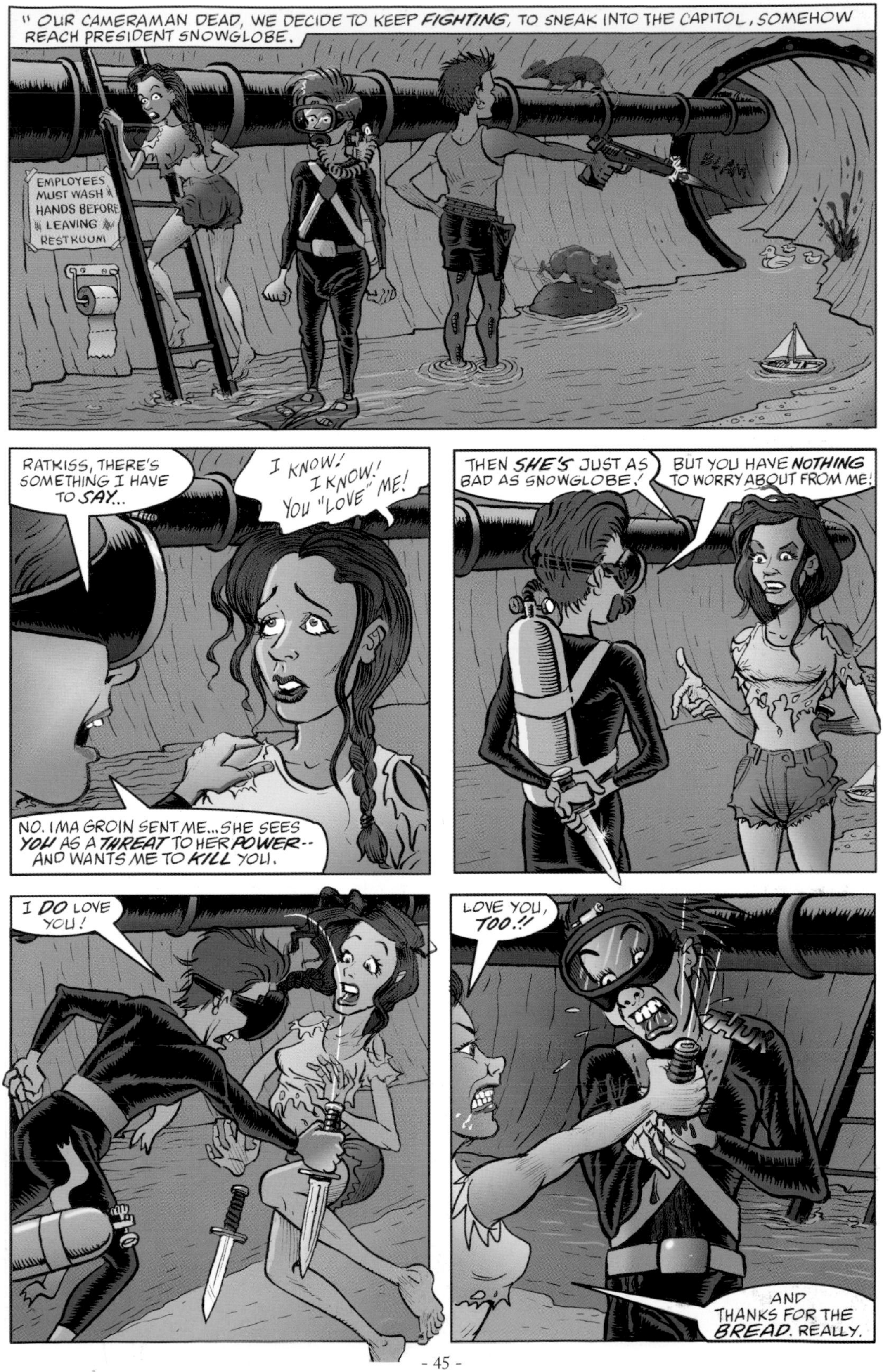
" OUR CAMERAMAN DEAD, WE DECIDE TO KEEP FIGHTING, TO SNEAK INTO THE CAPITOL, SOMEHOW REACH PRESIDENT SNOWGLOBE.
EMPLOYEES MUST WASH HANDS BEFORE LEAVING RESTROOM
BLAM
RATKISS, THERE'S SOMETHING I HAVE TO SAY...
I KNOW! I KNOW! YOU "LOVE" ME!
NO. IMA GROIN SENT ME... SHE SEES YOU AS A THREAT TO HER POWER-- AND WANTS ME TO KILL YOU.
THEN SHE'S JUST AS BAD AS SNOWGLOBE!
BUT YOU HAVE NOTHING TO WORRY ABOUT FROM ME!
I DO LOVE YOU!
LOVE YOU, TOO.!!
THUK
AND THANKS FOR THE BREAD. REALLY.

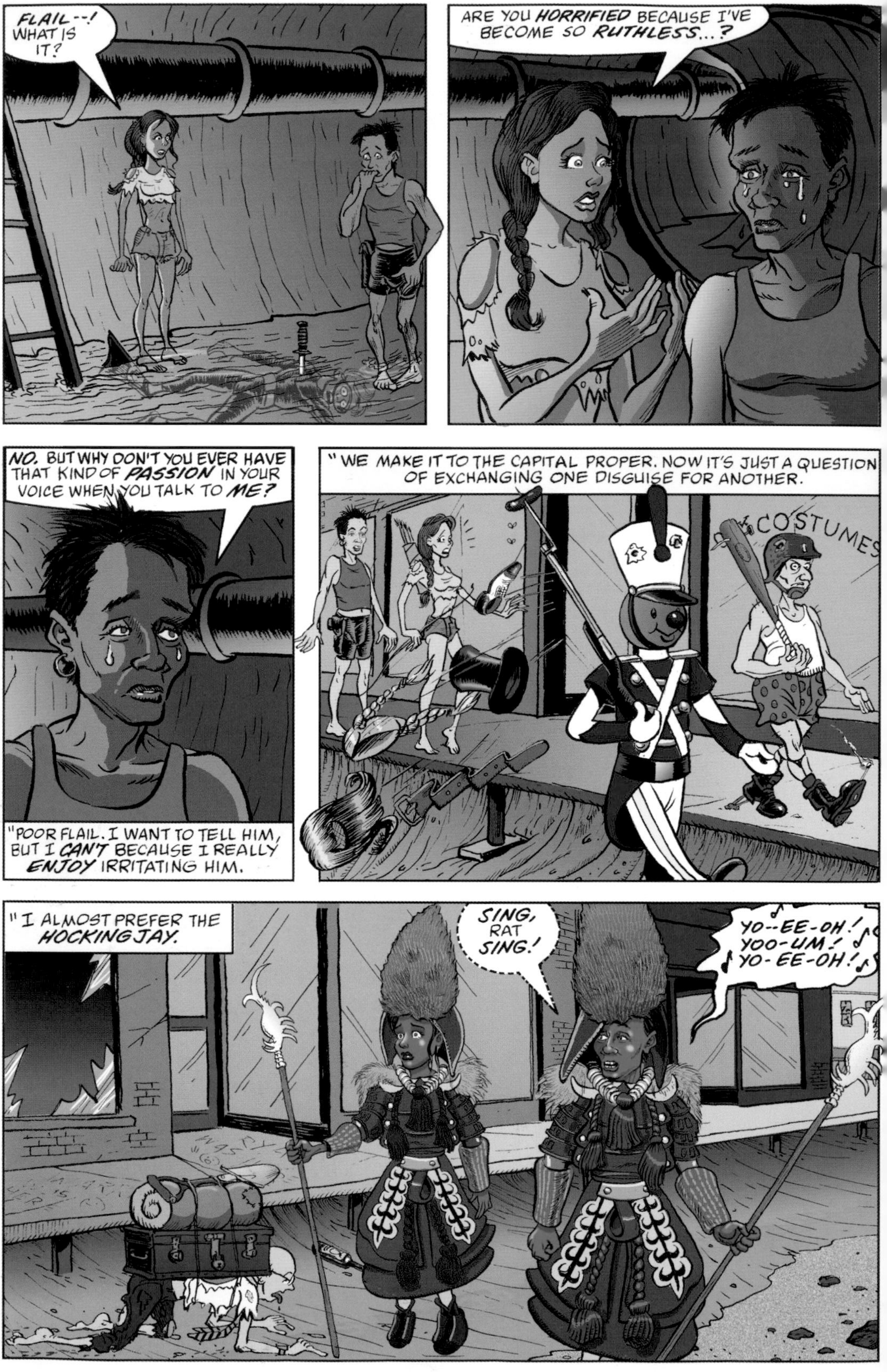
FLAIL--! WHAT IS IT?
ARE YOU HORRIFIED BECAUSE I'VE BECOME SO RUTHLESS...?
NO. BUT WHY DON'T YOU EVER HAVE THAT KIND OF PASSION IN YOUR VOICE WHEN YOU TALK TO ME?
"POOR FLAIL. I WANT TO TELL HIM, BUT I CAN'T BECAUSE I REALLY ENJOY IRRITATING HIM.
"WE MAKE IT TO THE CAPITAL PROPER. NOW IT'S JUST A QUESTION OF EXCHANGING ONE DISGUISE FOR ANOTHER.
COSTUMES
"I ALMOST PREFER THE HOCKINGJAY.
SING, RAT SING!
YO--EE-OH! YOO-UM! YO-EE-OH!

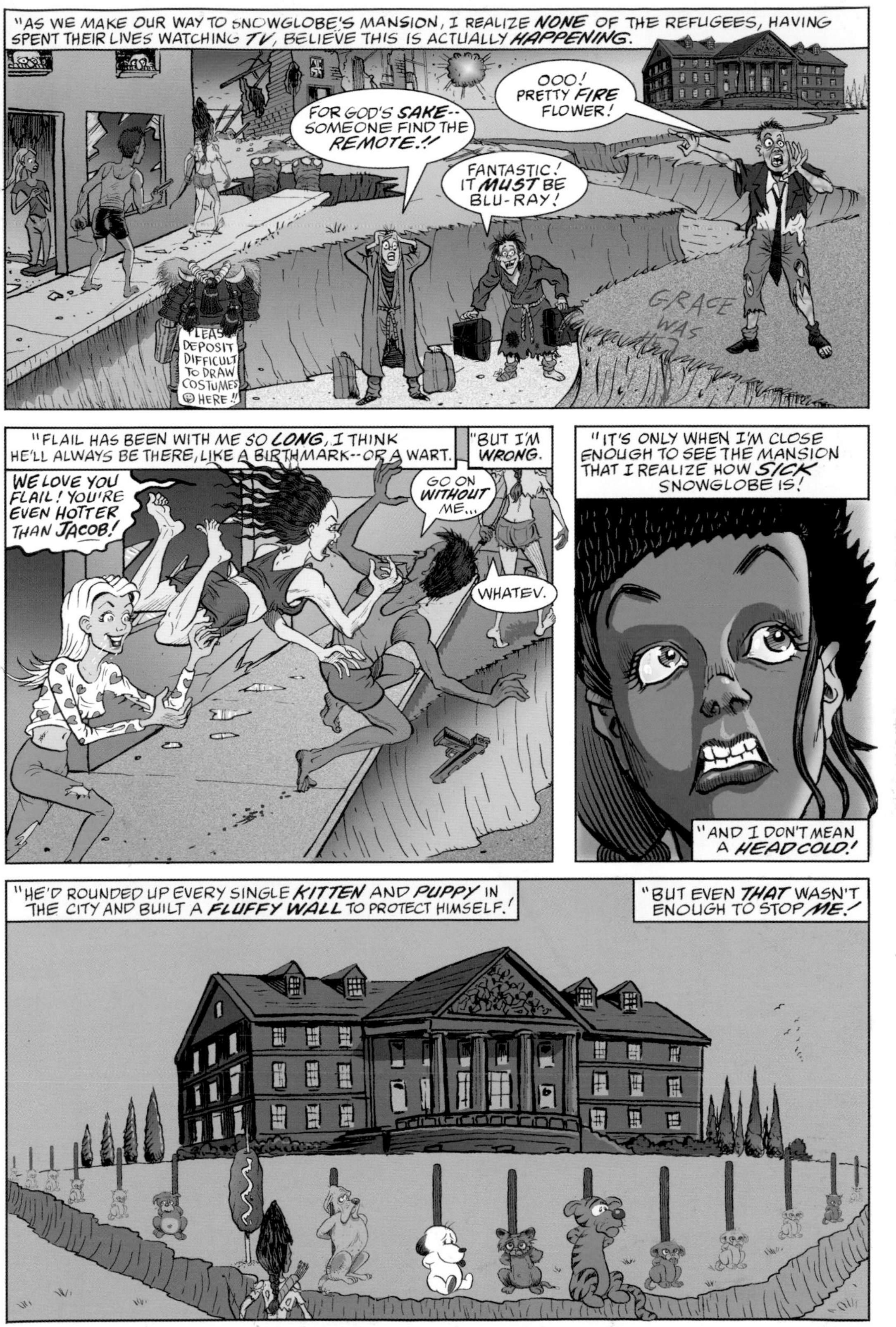
"AS WE MAKE OUR WAY TO SNOWGLOBE'S MANSION, I REALIZE NONE OF THE REFUGEES, HAVING SPENT THEIR LIVES WATCHING TV, BELIEVE THIS IS ACTUALLY HAPPENING.
FOR GOD'S SAKE-- SOMEONE FIND THE REMOTE.!!
FANTASTIC! IT MUST BE BLU-RAY!
OOO! PRETTY FIRE FLOWER!
LEASE DEPOSIT DIFFICULT TO DRAW COSTUMES HERE!!
GRACE WAS
"FLAIL HAS BEEN WITH ME SO LONG, I THINK HE'LL ALWAYS BE THERE, LIKE A BIRTHMARK--OR A WART.
"BUT I'M WRONG.
WE LOVE YOU FLAIL! YOU'RE EVEN HOTTER THAN JACOB!
GO ON WITHOUT ME...
WHATEV.
"IT'S ONLY WHEN I'M CLOSE ENOUGH TO SEE THE MANSION THAT I REALIZE HOW SICK SNOWGLOBE IS!
"AND I DON'T MEAN A HEADCOLD!
"HE'D ROUNDED UP EVERY SINGLE KITTEN AND PUPPY IN THE CITY AND BUILT A FLUFFY WALL TO PROTECT HIMSELF.
"BUT EVEN THAT WASN'T ENOUGH TO STOP ME.!

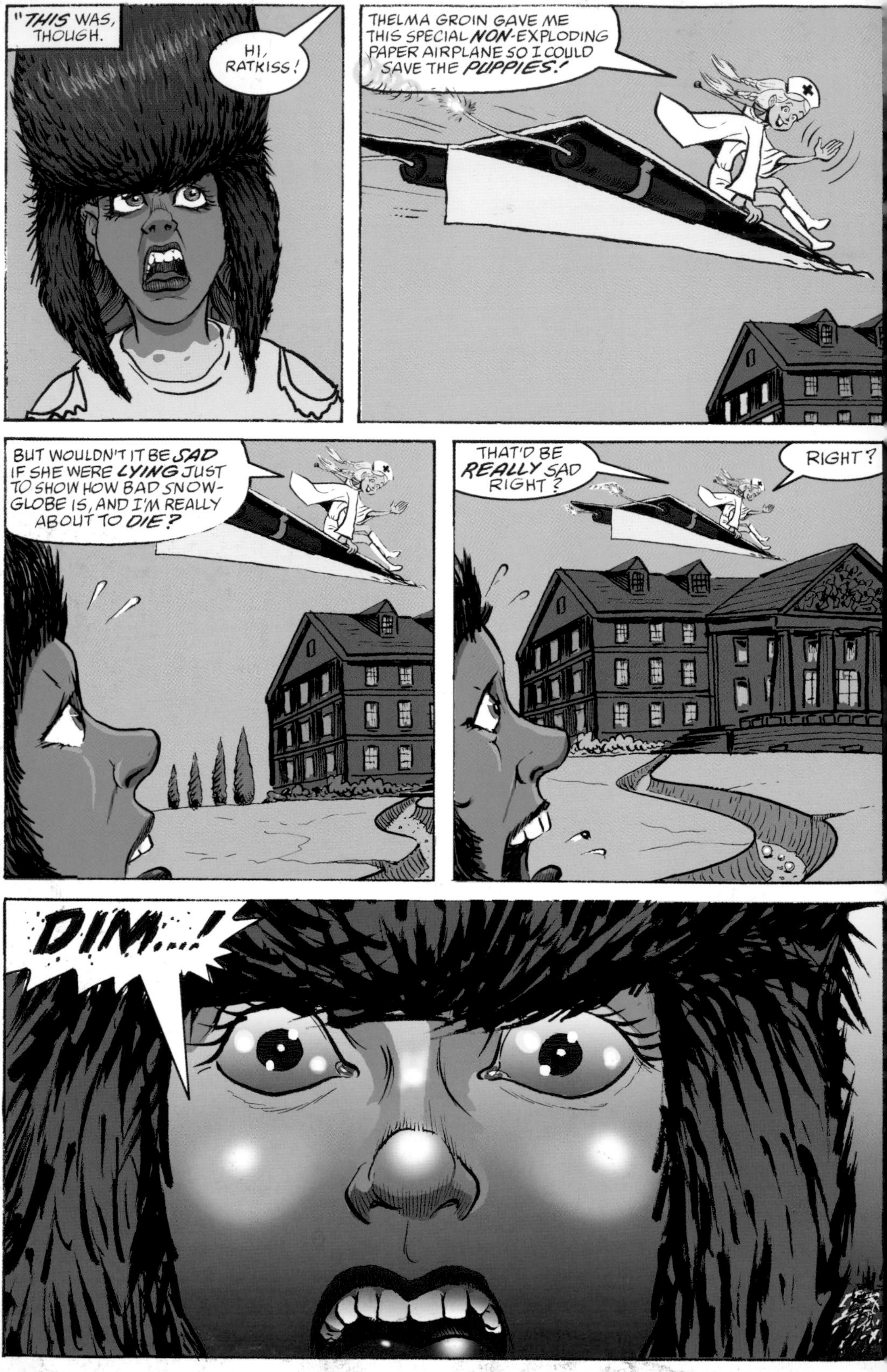
"THIS WAS, THOUGH.
HI, RATKISS!
THELMA GROIN GAVE ME THIS SPECIAL NON-EXPLODING PAPER AIRPLANE SO I COULD SAVE THE PUPPIES!
BUT WOULDN'T IT BE SAD IF SHE WERE LYING JUST TO SHOW HOW BAD SNOW-GLOBE IS, AND I'M REALLY ABOUT TO DIE?
THAT'D BE REALLY SAD RIGHT?
RIGHT?
DIM...!

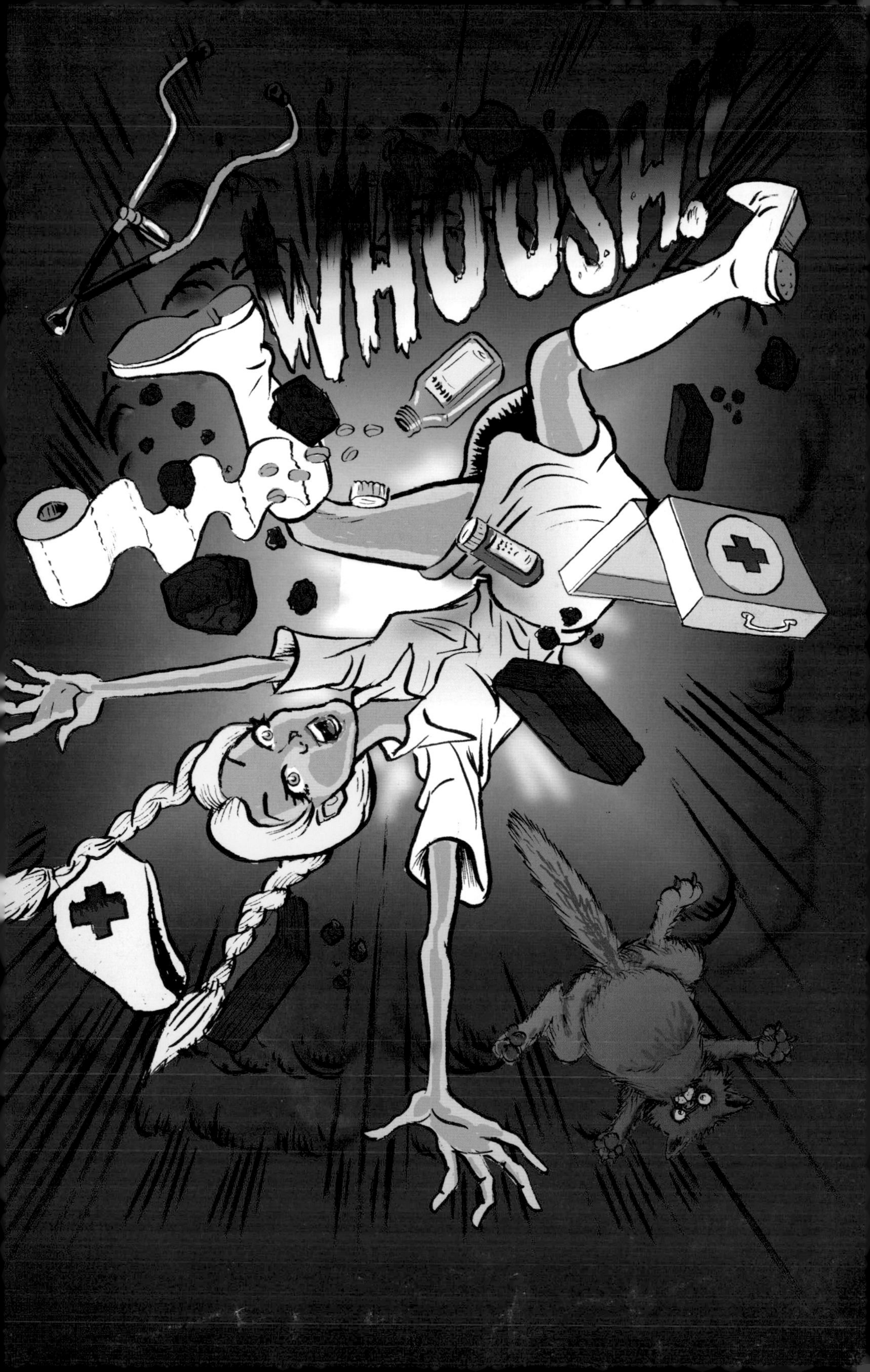
WHOOOSH!

"I DON'T KNOW HOW *LONG* I'M UNCONSCIOUS.

"I DON'T KNOW IF I EVER REALLY *WAS* CONSCIOUS.

"I MEAN, WHAT *IS* CONSCIOUSNESS, ANYWAY?

"MERE *AWARENESS?*

"..OR IS THERE A *SOUL?*

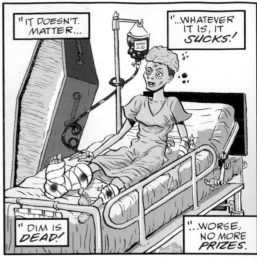

"IT DOESN'T. MATTER...

"..WHATEVER IT IS, IT *SUCKS!*

"DIM IS *DEAD!*

"..WORSE, NO MORE *PRIZES.*

"AS SOON AS I CAN *WALK,* I VISIT THE REBEL'S STAR *PRISONER,* THE FORMER *PRESIDENT SNOWGLOBE.*

"HE'S A CHANGED MAN-- NOT AS *FUNNY* AS HE *USED* TO BE...

WHAT IS WRONG WITH YOU PEOPLE?!! I KEPT TELLING YOU THE GAMES WERE OPTIONAL!!!

OPTIONAL!

NO ONE HAD TO *DIE.*

CRAZY KIDS.

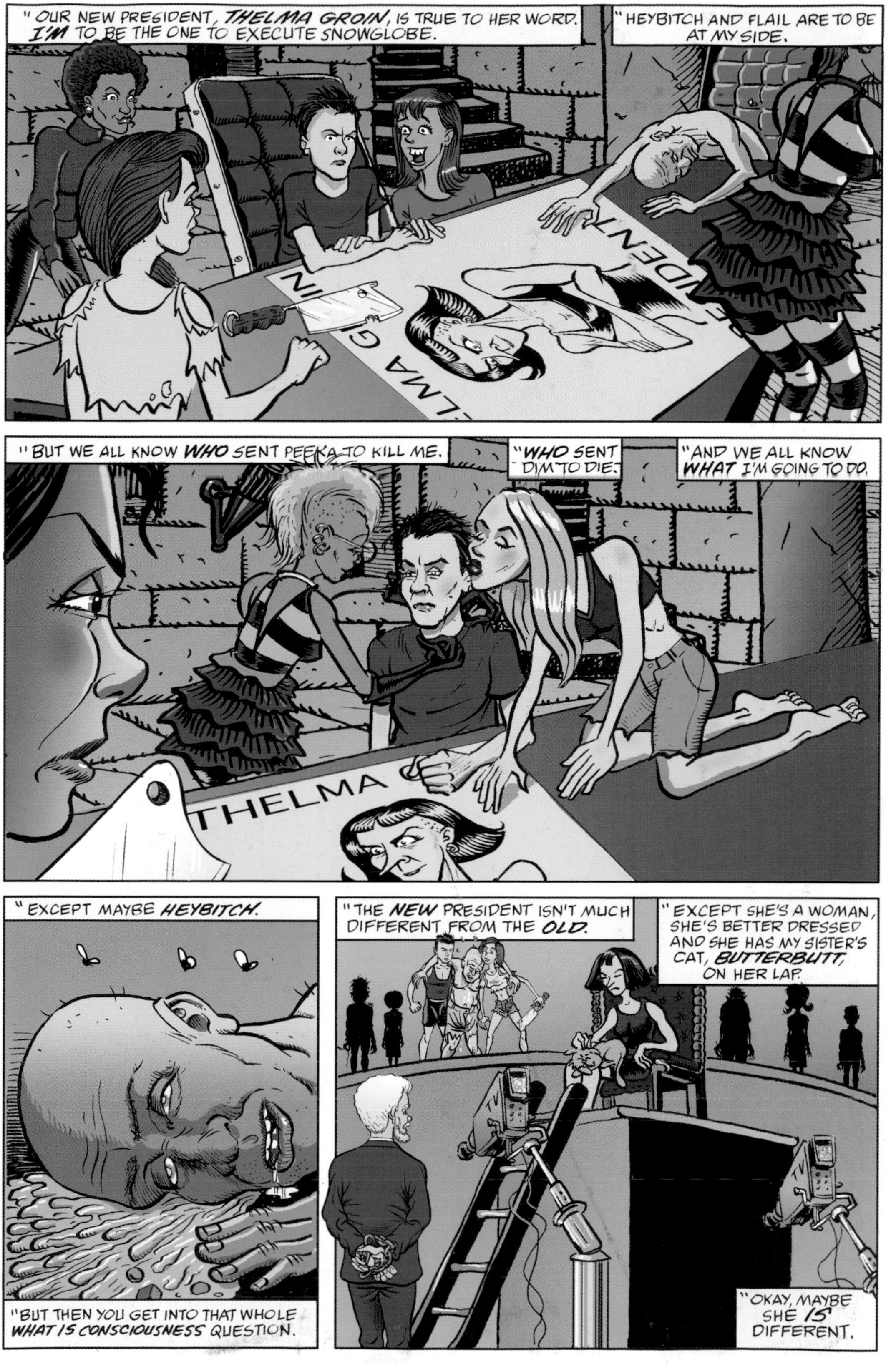
"OUR NEW PRESIDENT, THELMA GROIN, IS TRUE TO HER WORD. I'M TO BE THE ONE TO EXECUTE SNOWGLOBE.
"HEYBITCH AND FLAIL ARE TO BE AT MY SIDE.
THELMA GROIN
"BUT WE ALL KNOW WHO SENT PEEKA TO KILL ME.
"WHO SENT DIM TO DIE.
"AND WE ALL KNOW WHAT I'M GOING TO DO.
THELMA
"EXCEPT MAYBE HEYBITCH.
"BUT THEN YOU GET INTO THAT WHOLE WHAT IS CONSCIOUSNESS QUESTION.
"THE NEW PRESIDENT ISN'T MUCH DIFFERENT FROM THE OLD.
"EXCEPT SHE'S A WOMAN, SHE'S BETTER DRESSED AND SHE HAS MY SISTER'S CAT, BUTTERBUTT, ON HER LAP.
"OKAY, MAYBE SHE IS DIFFERENT.

"THERE HE IS, THE MOST *EVIL* MAN IN WHAT'S LEFT OF THE WORLD. I'M TO MAKE AN *EXAMPLE* OF HIM.

" WOULD IT BE ANY DIFFERENT FROM WHAT HE DID TO ME? ANY DIFFERENT FROM THE *GAMES?*

"YEAH... "*THIS* TIME THERE *AREN'T* ANY PRIZES!" "I *KNOW.*

"I ASKED. " *TWICE!*

"I DON'T KNOW *WHAT* FLAIL IS THINKING, PROBABLY THAT I'M PAYING TOO MUCH *ATTENTION* TO *SNOWGLOBE* NOW.

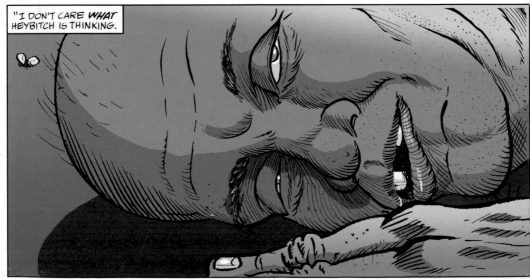

"I DON'T CARE *WHAT* HEYBITCH IS THINKING.

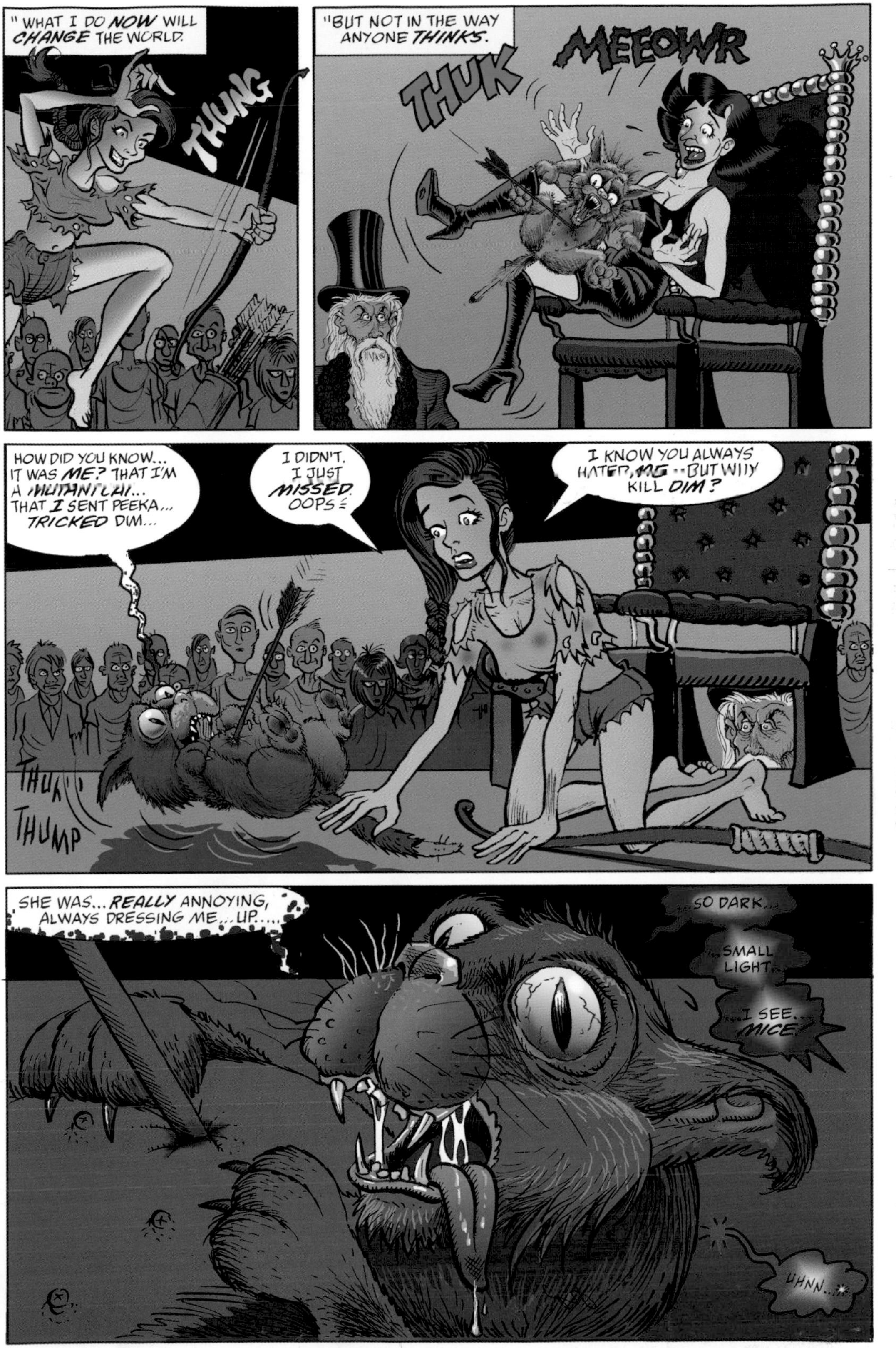
"WHAT I DO NOW WILL CHANGE THE WORLD.
THUNG
"BUT NOT IN THE WAY ANYONE THINKS.
THUK
MEEOWR
HOW DID YOU KNOW... IT WAS ME? THAT I'M A MUTANT CAT... THAT I SENT PEEKA... TRICKED DIM...
I DIDN'T. I JUST MISSED. OOPS
I KNOW YOU ALWAYS HATED ME... BUT WHY KILL DIM?
THUMP
SHE WAS... REALLY ANNOYING, ALWAYS DRESSING ME... UP....
SO DARK...
...SMALL LIGHT...
...I SEE... MICE
UHNN...

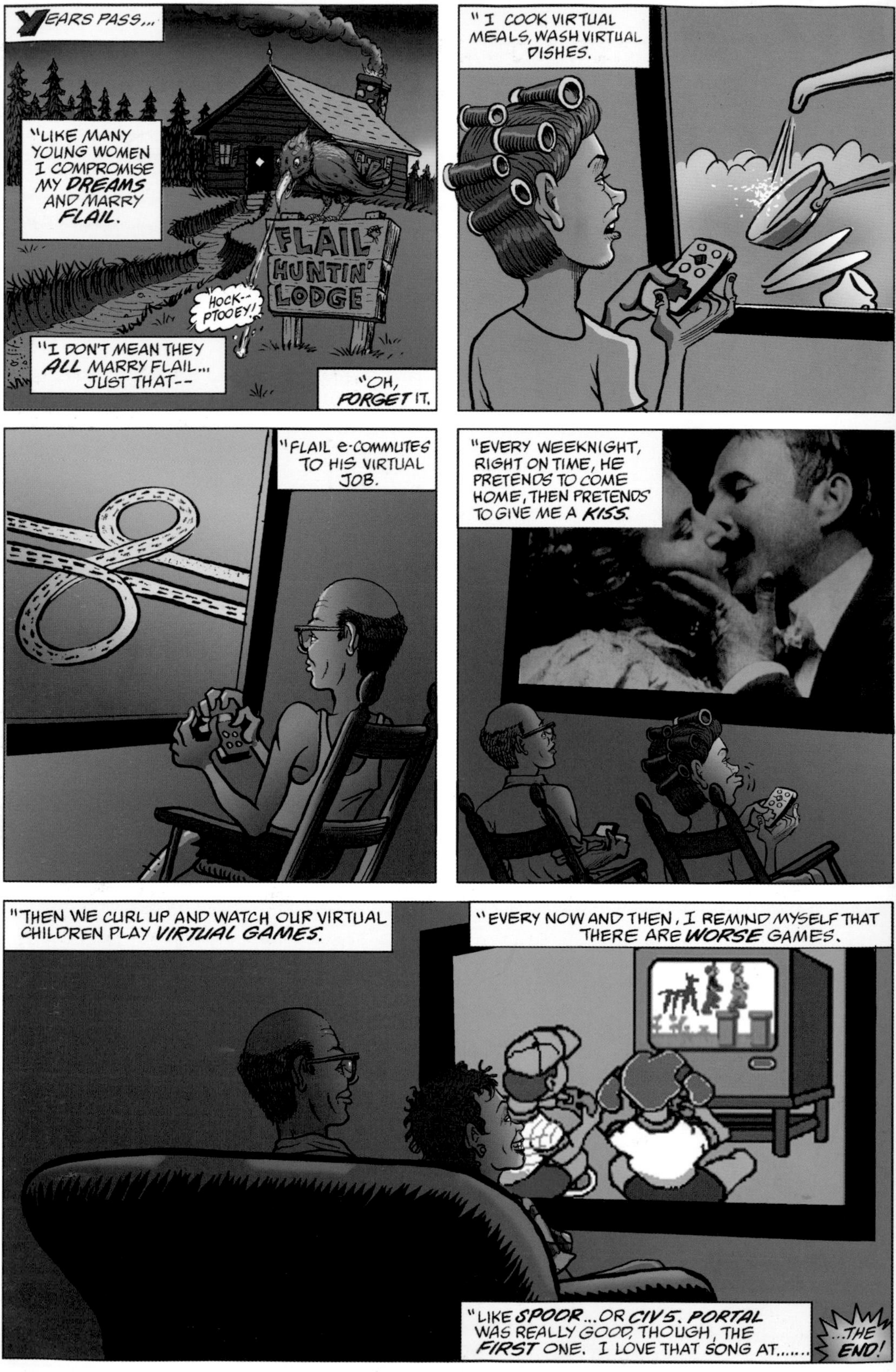
YEARS PASS...
"LIKE MANY YOUNG WOMEN I COMPROMISE MY DREAMS AND MARRY FLAIL.
FLAIL HUNTIN' LODGE
HOCK-- PTOOEY!
"I DON'T MEAN THEY ALL MARRY FLAIL... JUST THAT--
"OH, FORGET IT.
"I COOK VIRTUAL MEALS, WASH VIRTUAL DISHES.
"FLAIL e-COMMUTES TO HIS VIRTUAL JOB.
"EVERY WEEKNIGHT, RIGHT ON TIME, HE PRETENDS TO COME HOME, THEN PRETENDS TO GIVE ME A KISS.
"THEN WE CURL UP AND WATCH OUR VIRTUAL CHILDREN PLAY VIRTUAL GAMES.
"EVERY NOW AND THEN, I REMIND MYSELF THAT THERE ARE WORSE GAMES.
"LIKE SPOOR...OR CIV 5. PORTAL WAS REALLY GOOD, THOUGH, THE FIRST ONE. I LOVE THAT SONG AT......
...THE END!

WATCH OUT FOR PAPERCUTZ

Welcome to the facetious, felicific, and frightfully feral fourth volume of PAPERCUTZ SLICES, the critically acclaimed graphic novel series dedicated to painfully poking fun at your favorite pop culture phenomena. I'm Jim Salicrup, the son of a ditch-dweller and Papercutz Editor-in-Chief, here to thank you for buying this Papercutz graphic novel. You did buy it, didn't you? 'Cause if you didn't we'll hunt you down and kill you! Oh, it was a gift? Well, that's different. We won't kill you then. Although, you may die laughing at the all the jokes and funny pictures we managed to pack into this edition of PAPERCUTZ SLICES. If you haven't read "The Hunger Pains" yet, and you're some kind of weirdo who reads the text pages first, perhaps you might want to consider taking out a life insurance policy…? You can even name me as your beneficiary. That only seems fair.

If this is the first time you've encountered PAPERCUTZ SLICES, that leads me to ask—where the heck have you been? You missed the hilarious "Harry Potty and the Deathly Boring," the vampire and werewolf-filled "breaking down," and the mythical "Percy Jerkson and the Ovolactovegetarians," all by the satirical team supreme, Stefan Petrucha (and co-writers and daughters Maia Kinney-Petrucha and Margo Kinney-Petrucha) and Rick Parker. Stefan and Rick first rocketed to farcical fame in the pages of TALES FROM THE CRYPT #8 which featured their "Diary of a Stinky Dead Kid"! And they've been lampooning together ever since.

Now, there's no need to get even the slightest bit depressed about missing these landmark accomplishments in the highly specialized field of spoofery and unauthorized parody, 'cause each and everyone one of these PAPERCUTZ SLICES comic masterpieces is still available at your favorite bookseller (you know—bookstores, online booksellers, comicbook stores, book fairs, etc.) or directly from Papercutz (see details on page 2). There's even a special boxed set, featuring all three of the previous PAPERCUTZ SLICES volumes available now! And if that wasn't enough, we've got a super special announcement to make in the very next paragraph…

Super Special Announcement: Due to popular demand, you can now order every volume of PAPERCUTZ SLICES digitally from comiXology.com. Whether you have an iPad or a Kindle Fire or one of a gazillion other digital devices, you can now enjoy "Harry Potty," "Percy Jerkson," or even "Diary of a Stinky Dead Kid," digitally. So, that should make all you gadget geeks super-happy!

So, while we still have your attention, may we direct it to the Papercutz excerpts and previews on the following pages…? We figure if you liked the mindless mayhem of "The Hunger Pains," then you'll love the Spinjitzu action in the pages of LEGO® NINJAGO. It's on sale now and available at booksellers everywhere. LEGO® NINJAGO features the exciting tales of four ninja battling the craziest foes you've ever seen. Written by Greg Farshtey, and illustrated by Paulo Henrigue, it's ninjas in the LEGO® style!

There's no room left to tell you what'll be Stefan and Rick's target for PAPERCUTZ SLICES #5, so you'll have to keep an eye on www.papercutz.com for future announcements. So, until we meet again-- May the Farce be with you!

Jim

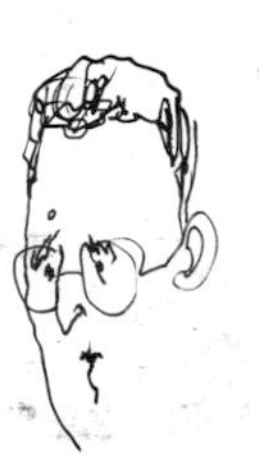

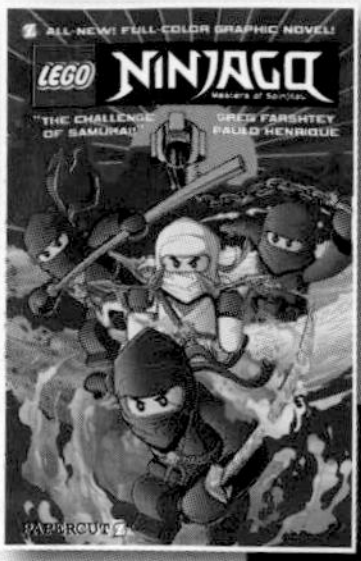
LEGO
NINJAGO
PAPERCUTZ

Special preview of LEGO® NINJANGO #1
"The Challenge of Samukai!"

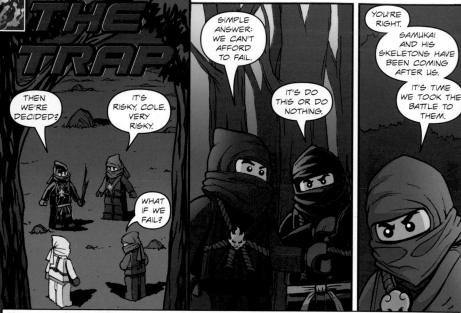

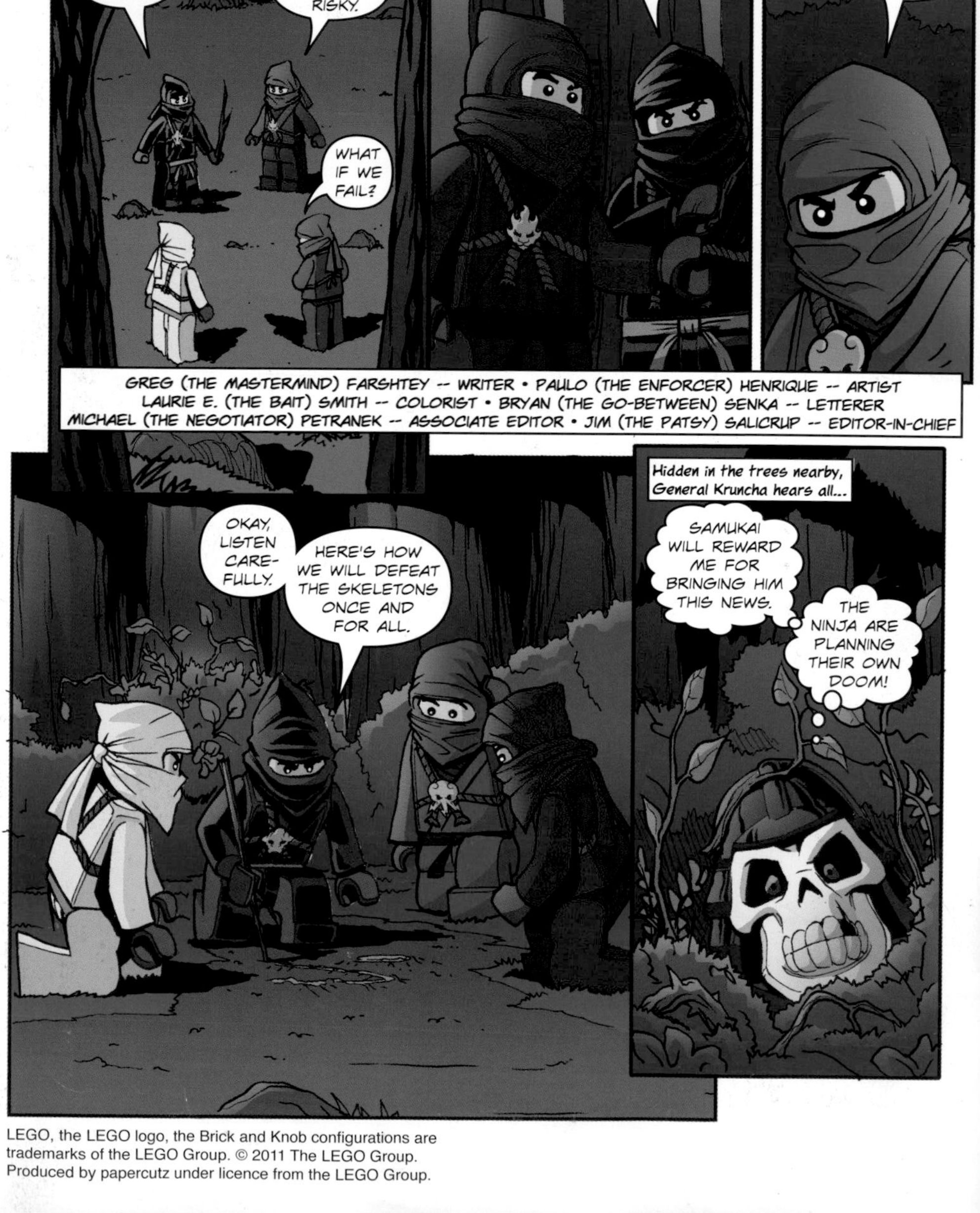
THE TRAP
THEN WE'RE DECIDED?
IT'S RISKY, COLE. VERY RISKY.
WHAT IF WE FAIL?
SIMPLE ANSWER: WE CAN'T AFFORD TO FAIL.
IT'S DO THIS OR DO NOTHING.
YOU'RE RIGHT.
SAMUKAI AND HIS SKELETONS HAVE BEEN COMING AFTER US.
IT'S TIME WE TOOK THE BATTLE TO THEM.
GREG (THE MASTERMIND) FARSHTEY -- WRITER • PAULO (THE ENFORCER) HENRIQUE -- ARTIST
LAURIE E. (THE BAIT) SMITH -- COLORIST • BRYAN (THE GO-BETWEEN) SENKA -- LETTERER
MICHAEL (THE NEGOTIATOR) PETRANEK -- ASSOCIATE EDITOR • JIM (THE PATSY) SALICRUP -- EDITOR-IN-CHIEF
OKAY, LISTEN CARE-FULLY.
HERE'S HOW WE WILL DEFEAT THE SKELETONS ONCE AND FOR ALL.
Hidden in the trees nearby, General Kruncha hears all...
SAMUKAI WILL REWARD ME FOR BRINGING HIM THIS NEWS.
THE NINJA ARE PLANNING THEIR OWN DOOM!

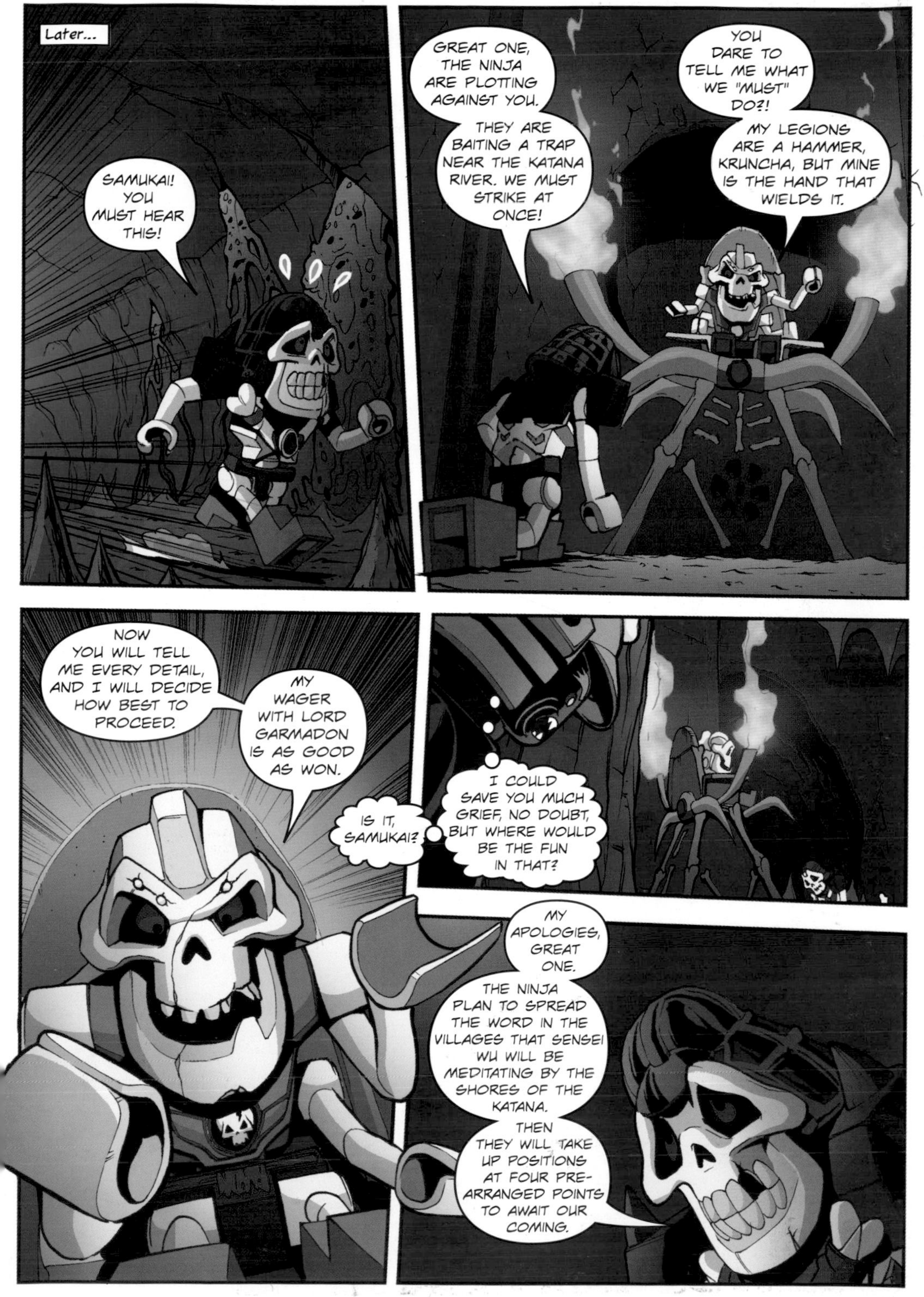
Later...
SAMUKAI! YOU MUST HEAR THIS!
GREAT ONE, THE NINJA ARE PLOTTING AGAINST YOU.
THEY ARE BAITING A TRAP NEAR THE KATANA RIVER. WE MUST STRIKE AT ONCE!
YOU DARE TO TELL ME WHAT WE "MUST" DO?!
MY LEGIONS ARE A HAMMER, KRUNCHA, BUT MINE IS THE HAND THAT WIELDS IT.
NOW YOU WILL TELL ME EVERY DETAIL, AND I WILL DECIDE HOW BEST TO PROCEED.
MY WAGER WITH LORD GARMADON IS AS GOOD AS WON.
IS IT, SAMUKAI?
I COULD SAVE YOU MUCH GRIEF, NO DOUBT, BUT WHERE WOULD BE THE FUN IN THAT?
MY APOLOGIES, GREAT ONE.
THE NINJA PLAN TO SPREAD THE WORD IN THE VILLAGES THAT SENSEI WU WILL BE MEDITATING BY THE SHORES OF THE KATANA.
THEN THEY WILL TAKE UP POSITIONS AT FOUR PRE-ARRANGED POINTS TO AWAIT OUR COMING.

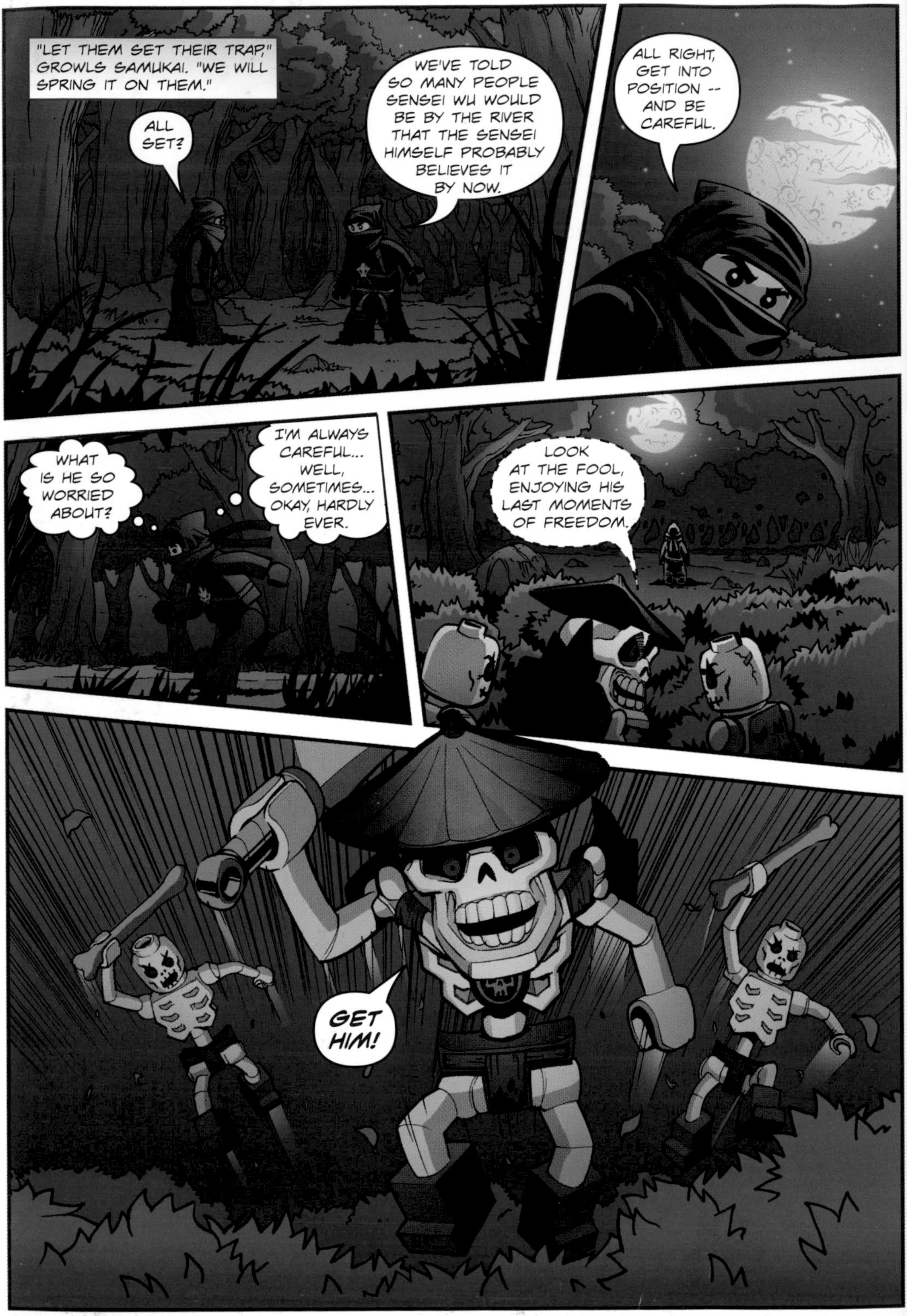
"LET THEM SET THEIR TRAP," GROWLS SAMUKAI. "WE WILL SPRING IT ON THEM."
ALL SET?
WE'VE TOLD SO MANY PEOPLE SENSEI WU WOULD BE BY THE RIVER THAT THE SENSEI HIMSELF PROBABLY BELIEVES IT BY NOW.
ALL RIGHT, GET INTO POSITION -- AND BE CAREFUL.
WHAT IS HE SO WORRIED ABOUT?
I'M ALWAYS CAREFUL... WELL, SOMETIMES... OKAY, HARDLY EVER.
LOOK AT THE FOOL, ENJOYING HIS LAST MOMENTS OF FREEDOM.
GET HIM!

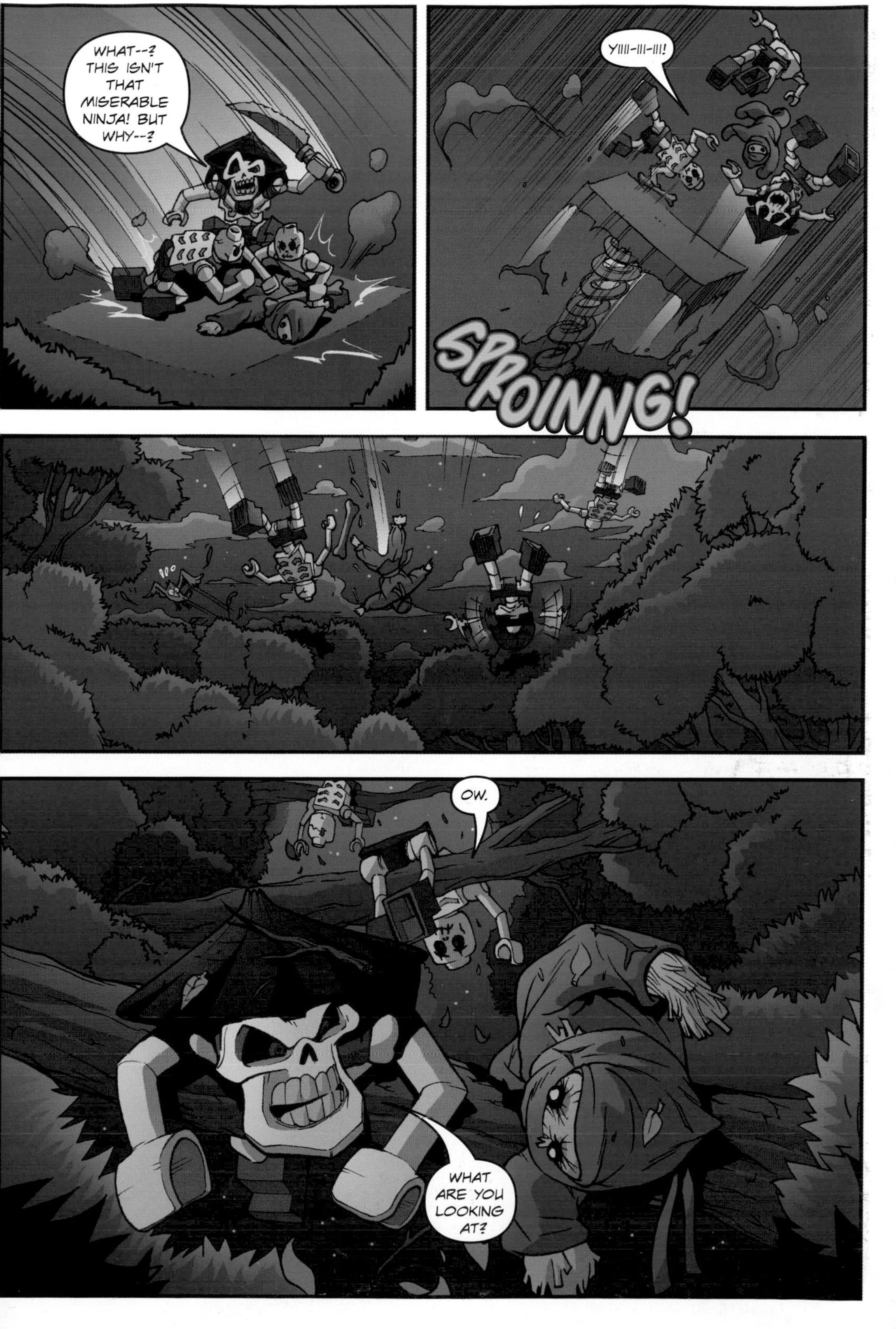

WHAT--? THIS ISN'T THAT MISERABLE NINJA! BUT WHY--?
YIIII-III-III!
SPROINNG!
OW.
WHAT ARE YOU LOOKING AT?

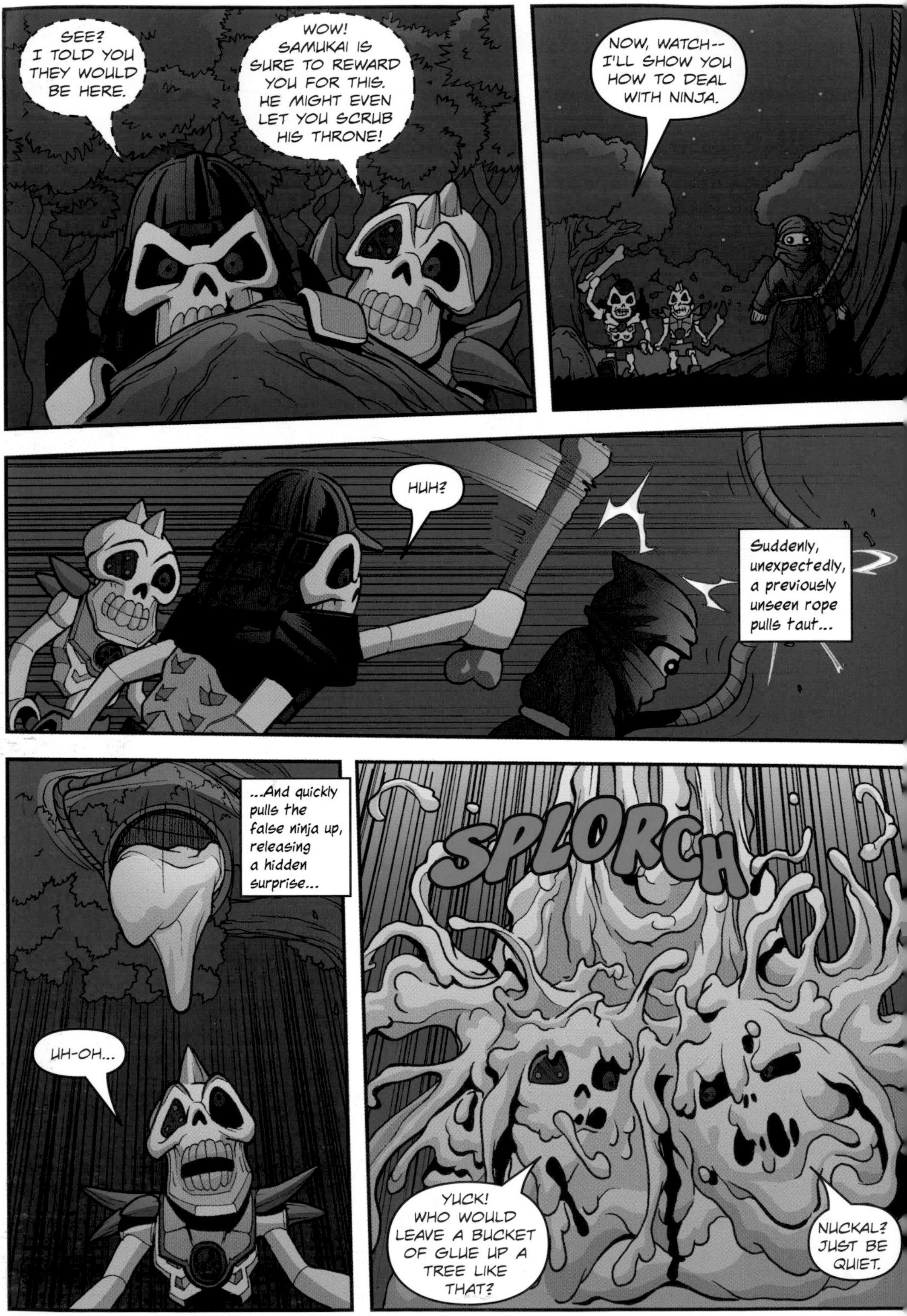
SEE? I TOLD YOU THEY WOULD BE HERE.
WOW! SAMUKAI IS SURE TO REWARD YOU FOR THIS. HE MIGHT EVEN LET YOU SCRUB HIS THRONE!
NOW, WATCH-- I'LL SHOW YOU HOW TO DEAL WITH NINJA.
HUH?
Suddenly, unexpectedly, a previously unseen rope pulls taut...
...And quickly pulls the false ninja up, releasing a hidden surprise...
UH-OH...
SPLORCH
YUCK! WHO WOULD LEAVE A BUCKET OF GLUE UP A TREE LIKE THAT?
NUCKAL? JUST BE QUIET.

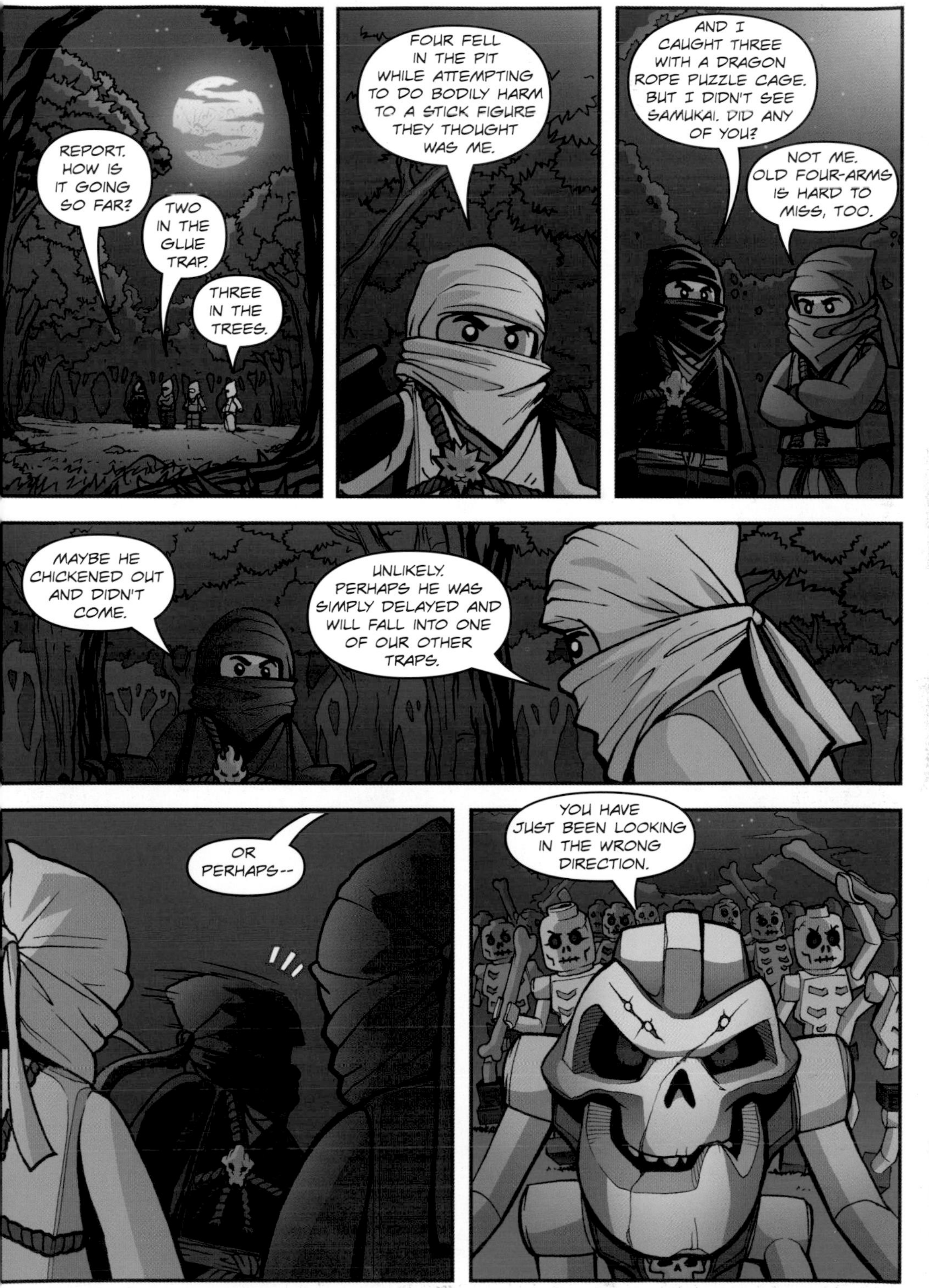
REPORT. HOW IS IT GOING SO FAR?
TWO IN THE GLUE TRAP.
THREE IN THE TREES.
FOUR FELL IN THE PIT WHILE ATTEMPTING TO DO BODILY HARM TO A STICK FIGURE THEY THOUGHT WAS ME.
AND I CAUGHT THREE WITH A DRAGON ROPE PUZZLE CAGE. BUT I DIDN'T SEE SAMUKAI. DID ANY OF YOU?
NOT ME. OLD FOUR-ARMS IS HARD TO MISS, TOO.
MAYBE HE CHICKENED OUT AND DIDN'T COME.
UNLIKELY. PERHAPS HE WAS SIMPLY DELAYED AND WILL FALL INTO ONE OF OUR OTHER TRAPS.
OR PERHAPS--
YOU HAVE JUST BEEN LOOKING IN THE WRONG DIRECTION.

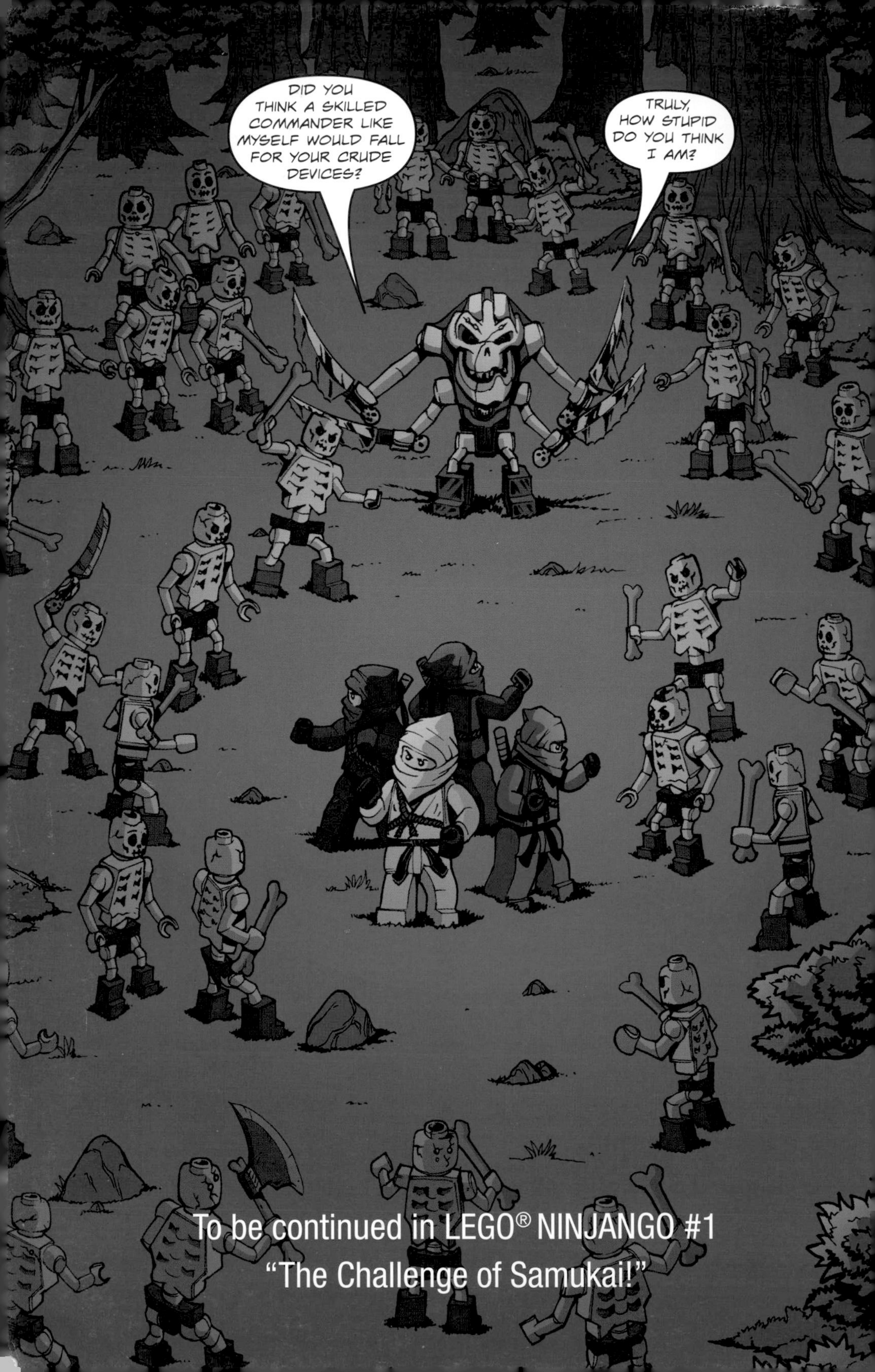
DID YOU THINK A SKILLED COMMANDER LIKE MYSELF WOULD FALL FOR YOUR CRUDE DEVICES?
TRULY, HOW STUPID DO YOU THINK I AM?
To be continued in LEGO® NINJANGO #1
"The Challenge of Samukai!"

LOTS MOE FUN!

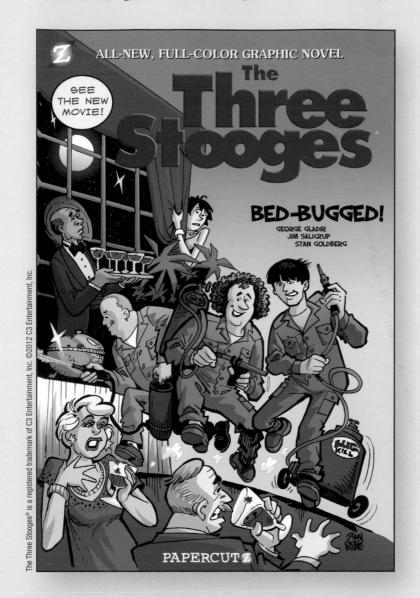

PLUS: LARRY AND CURLY FUN AT NO EXTRA COST!

Available Now at Booksellers Everywhere!

Think Inside the Box
Get the Boxed Set of Papercutz Slices #1-3!

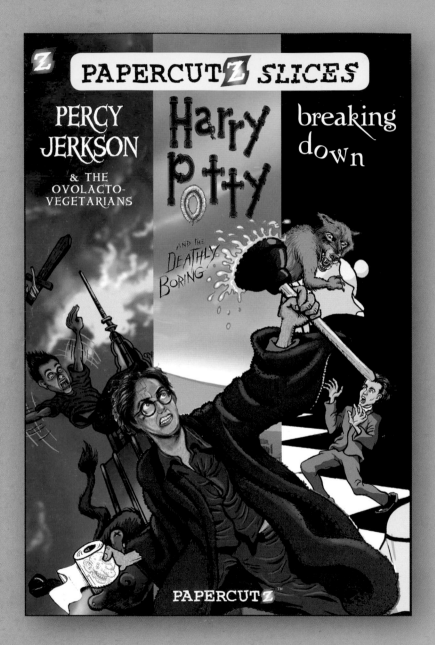